Death up t

Elizabeth Oakey

The Mrs Mortimer Mysteries

Death Up The Aisle
Death in Heels
Death in Tweed

and Death First Class (coming soon)

Paperback ISBN 978 0 9876441 8 3

Ebook ISBN 978 0 9876441 9 0

Prologue

This is the story of my wedding, honeymoon and the events that followed, which ultimately made me the woman I am today. And whether that's a good or a bad thing is neither here nor there, because here we are.

You will notice a couple of chapters that I allowed my aunt to write. I should point out that her thoughts on my wardrobe and coiffure do not tally with mine, and I cannot comment on her dealings with the police.

Kind regards,

Georgiana Mortimer

P.S. I should mention that some of the names of the people I encountered have been changed, and some have been added to my diary since my release. (One does not write full names whilst under lock and key. There is a certain etiquette to be observed *inside*, as I'm sure you can imagine.)

One

Although it was warm enough inside, there was a smattering of frost on the window pane. It was Christmas Eve morning — and my wedding day.

And I would like to think that it's because I am a favourite of my Aunt Bathsheba, that she decided to share her thoughts with me, as she did.

'You know, you don't have to go through with it, Georgiana. Edward's so old. Give it ten years and you'll be in your prime and he'll have lost his stamina.'

'Edward isn't ancient, Auntie B,' I said, adding an 'Ow!' for good measure, while she attacked my curls with a brush.

'In this day and age, there's no good reason to get married at all,' she said. 'Look at my Girls! All useful, intelligent, interesting members of society and not a wedding ring between them.'

'You're not talking about your daughters-in-law now, are you?'

'Absolutely not! And I should point out that their weddings at the abbey were the social events of those three seasons.' I flinched under her brush, but she carried on, vigorously. 'And their nuptials certainly weren't held out of sight, on Christmas Eve of all days. No, I am talking about my little team – my Girls. My Writers. It's not as if Bettina, Lettice and Jacqueline don't have fun! In fact, they possibly have too much fun. A decade older than you are, and not a single one of them married!'

My Aunt Bathsheba is the head of a small publishing house, which sells books about ladies, written by ladies for ladies, and their chief ingredient is pleasure, fun and frolics of some sort or other – as far as I can tell.

'I'm not sure that Lettice has a lot of fun,' I remarked.

'Miss Armstrong couldn't write the historical romances she does, if she didn't have a romp every now and again.'

'Well, I wouldn't know, would I? I've never got my hands on any of the books you publish, let alone Lettice's. Never been allowed t-aaagh!' I yelped as the brush's stiff bristles caught my ear.

'Oops-a-daisy!' she said, 'Well, they are tricky to find.'

'Not difficult to get hold of for the woman who publishes them though, surely? If I'm ever lucky enough t-'

'Lucky? To read those books?' said my aunt's maid, who was doing up the hundred-and-one pretty, little buttons on my silken sleeves.

'That's enough, Maude! Your opinion was not sought, and I can't begin to imagine how you managed to get your hands on them,' she said, as she plonked the veil on my head, forgetting the little comb that held it in place. While I wailed, my aunt began reminiscing about how much more civilised it was before the war, when there would have been countless highly competent maids available to see to my hair, and I had to agree.

I took a deep breath and thanked the two ladies for their help, and my aunt pointed out that if my hair were a proper length, it wouldn't have hurt so much. While I examined my reflection, she peered at the earrings my fiancé had given me – an early Christmas present. 'Whatever my thoughts on your husband-to-be, he certainly appears to have good taste in baubles.' And as she held them up to the light, there was the sound of uneven footsteps, something was knocked over, there was a curse or two, and one of my aunt's writers ambled in.

'Talking of too much fun…' I said.

Jack's hair was sticking up, her suit was in disarray and, with inky fingers, she fished a cigar out of her top pocket. 'Love the get-up, doll. Going anywhere fancy, Georgie?'

'Jacqueline!' complained my aunt, 'You know very well what we're doing here AND why Georgiana is wearing white!'

She sniggered in response, and bit the tip of her cigar. 'That dress is off-white – and I was just saying how fine Georgie looks!'

'And do not smoke that in here!'

'What do you mean in here? This is my home!' said Jack, with a grin.

'In a matter of hours, Georgiana's fiancé, will be her husband, and his flat will be theirs, so you're going to have to return to whatever arrangement you enjoyed previous to this one,' said my aunt. 'And what are you wearing, Jacqueline? Just look at the state of you!'

'I think I make a wonderful flatmate,' she said, searching her pockets for her lighter. 'And as for what I'm wearing, navy pinstripe is about the smartest thing there is.'

'I don't know what you've been up to, Miss Fabre,' said my aunt, 'But I am still waiting for the last ten chapters of the third book of the Rodeo Romances, and that get-up is not suitable for a church. You look like you've come straight from a poker club!'

'I have not come straight from a poker club,' said Jack, scraping her heavy fringe back. 'I've come straight from a mah-jong club, and that's a very different thing. I had a fine breakfast there and I'm ready for anything, although a cup of black tea wouldn't go amiss.'

Aunt Bathsheba asked Maude to bring us a fresh pot of tea and, for a couple of minutes at least, while we waited for the Ceylon to brew, we were all left to our own thoughts.

It was Jack who broke the silence. 'So how did you meet him anyway?'

'Huh?'

'Johnny. The old groomio. How did you meet him?'

'Johnny was the other one,' said Maude, taking away the empty pot, 'This one's Eddy.'

'His name is Edward Mortimer, and we met on a hiking trip in Pembrokeshire,' I said, taking a sip of my tea. 'The weather was pretty awful, but some of the girls from work had decided they were going to ramble through the Brecon Beacons. I was at a bit of a loose end, so I joined them. Agnes can be very persuasive. Anyway, after a couple of nights in hostels, and days hiking in driving rain, I'd had enough. So, while the other girls marched out of the pub, I stayed by the fire. My boots were soaked through, there was a stop a hundred yards up the road, and the landlady had told me there was a bus due in an hour's time. Another table of ramblers had just finished their round of leek and potato soup, and they were all heading back out too – all except one. His boots weren't wet through, but he obviously felt the same way I did about trampling about in the rain. He was charming, he wore natty tweeds, and he said we'd met before. At a racetrack somewhere.'

'The dogs?'

'No, Jack! It was horse racing. Anyway, the afternoon went on very nicely, we took the bus together – and here we are.'

'Here we are, indeed,' said my aunt, trying to catch my eye while I busied myself with my veil.

Mine is the generation who has been left behind, rapidly being forgotten. There aren't many available men my age in 1927 – and of course, there never will be, if you really think about it, but I went on a hike with a gaggle of female friends and managed to bag myself a well-dressed man with a nice smile and expensive shoes. My husband-to-be, Edward Mortimer is older than I am, of course, by a good fifteen years or more, and three months after we met, we were engaged, the banns had been read and the wedding was to be held at the Church of Saint Xavier's on Christmas Eve. Why not? And yet... I glanced out of the window and the sight of the trees being knocked about by a chill wind sent shivers across my shoulders. We could surely have waited until the spring.

I recalled Edward joking that I might find someone else before then, and that he wanted me all to himself, so I had acquiesced. I finished my tea.

'Time is galloping along,' said my aunt. 'And I have to pick up my hat before we head for the church. I am supposed to be there before you, after all, and you know how your uncle feels about tardiness. Now, time for the tiara!'

I regarded the box my aunt handed to me and, glancing at the writing on the card attached to it, I noticed that it wasn't Edward's, and I could only assume that his nanny was in charge of this little request too. I wondered how I would manage Nanny's "little boy" once he was married – and I also wondered how the woman would keep herself busy without him.

Something about my expression must have changed, because when Aunt Bathsheba next spoke, all her bluster was gone. 'You know, you're still very welcome to borrow one of the family tiaras. I've at least three of them stowed away in the bank down the road, and it wouldn't take me any time at all to go and fetch one.'

'No, no, Auntie Sheba, it's not that,' I said, shaking my head, and trying hard to muster a smile.

She gave my shoulder a squeeze, and everything about the look on her face, and the silence that followed, said 'If you marry him, you marry him, and I shall do my very best to say nothing more on the matter.'

And if I walked away? I suspected my aunt would say even less, and we would move on even more quickly.

Maude returned with the topped-up teapot and I opened the box. While it may indeed have been true that it was one of Edward's late mother's prized possessions, my aunt tried to look suitably awestruck, but the expression on her face told me that she doubted those were real diamonds and sapphires. And I couldn't help but agree.

Two

'Where did you get that? asked Jack, making a face. She wasn't one of my aunt's more subtle employees.

'It belonged to Edward's mother,' I said. 'Sheba and I bumped into Nanny when she brought it round to the apartment yesterday.'

Despite the fact that Nanny hadn't bathed a babe in at least forty years, her hair was as firmly pinned back as it would have been the first day of her employ, and she wore not a scrap of face powder. The woman (whose actual name, I hadn't the slightest idea of) had passed me the box – with a disapproving pout – and left the suitcase on the doorstep, saying it was freshly packed for "her boy". And without another word, Nanny had entered the lift, the doors had closed after her and she was off! The case contained new half-hose, pyjamas and a couple of pressed and fiercely starched tunic shirts.

'Well, I may not have a trousseau, but it seems that my fiancé does!' I'd remarked, and my aunt had reminded me that she would have been happy to rustle up some cotton and silk whatnots if I'd wanted them.

Much as I would have liked (and frankly needed) a whole new wardrobe, my aunt and uncle had already done so much for me.

As the parents of three boys, they said they'd got away lightly when it came to wedding expenses, and I was very grateful for their generosity. They were kind enough to cover the cost of my nuptials because there was so little chance of my parents stumping up for them. The less said about my father, the better, and my mother – the Honourable Margaret Godfrey? She is my Uncle Lawrence's sister, although since her move to Mexico, she prefers to be known as "Margareta Reyezuelo". She popped over for a quick visit a couple of months ago, and she's been staying with my aunt and uncle, and it was sheer chance that her visit coincided with the wedding.

Our tea finished, I checked my parting and popped the tiara on my head. My aunt and Jack both nodded in an encouraging manner, while Maude ran her finger along the top of the wardrobe, and we heard the sound of distant bells. 'Time to go, ma'am,' she said, wiping her hands on her skirt. 'Up we get, chop-chop!' While I gathered myself, Maude turned to me with a wide smile. 'Look at you. All grown up!'

I laughed and reminded her of my 28 years of age.

'Yes, well –' and Maude was good enough not to say the words, "better late than never". Instead, she asked, 'So, what's your "Something old, something new, something borrowed, something blue", Miss Wren?'

'She won't be "Miss Georgiana Wren" for much longer,' said my aunt.

'Ridiculous convention,' said Jack, stubbing out her cigar. 'Fancy changing your name for somebody!'

'"Mortimer" is a perfectly nice name, and I'm very happy to be a "Mrs"! And, for your information, my something old is the tiara, and my something new is the frock.'

It had been designed by a friend of mine, Hermione Russell, who is a close friend of Cecil Beaton. It was a beautiful little number in oyster georgette, with full-length sleeves to ensure that I didn't shiver at the altar. My aunt had thought the hem too low, and the neckline far too high, and asked me where the bustle was. She wasn't sure about the pockets I'd insisted on, either.

'And the something borrowed?' asked Maude.

'This little green purse was what Auntie Sheba wore when she married Uncle Lawrence, so I'm borrowing that, and I'm borrowing the something-to-keep-me-warm from them too.'

Christmas Eve was bound to be freezing, of course, and after rifling through Bathsheba's winter wardrobe and trying a few pieces on, I had an odd little selection to pick from, including a duffel coat, a fox fur shoulder-to-ankle number Bathsheba had worn as a debutante, and a selection of capes. After giving them all a sniff, I chose an opera cape that was dark green velvet. Quite festive really.

And the something blue? That was the sapphires on the tiara that had been delivered.

'And something scented?' said Jack, offering me one of her cigars.

'Yes, well, as Maude said, we really should be going,' said my aunt, fiddling with my veil again. 'We have to pick up my hat and stole on the way to the church, from the lady who lifts my hems and sees to my seams. She's changing the band and pepping up the fur. We shall see you at Saint Xavier's, Georgiana, and don't be too late if you can help it. You know how your Uncle Lawrence is about punctuality!'

I nodded, and reapplied my lipstick, and I couldn't help noticing how pale I looked, and my aunt must have thought the same, because she told me that a bit more rouge wouldn't go amiss. Nerves were getting the better of me, my tummy was turning cartwheels. I rubbed the diamond on my engagement ring, and did my best to focus on the day ahead – and not question that stone's authenticity too.

'You look lovely, my dear,' said my aunt, before turning towards the hall and calling, 'Jack? JACK! Are you ready to go? Where are you? Lawrence will be here soon – he's taking Georgiana off to the church, and we have to get there before she does!'

Jack shouted back that she'd be with us in a minute, although how she was going to spruce herself up to go to a wedding, I couldn't imagine. We had lived together for a month, and she hadn't worn anything in any of that time that would have been socially acceptable. And so it was, that a minute later, she returned, wearing a different tie – and a leather jacket and helmet.

'You aren't!' said my aunt.

'I am! I'm on my bike, and it's no good wearing a dress with leathers.'

'Jacqueline, you know very well I would never expect you to wear a dress. I'm long past demanding that of you, but a pair of clean trousers that have been freshly-pressed, might have been a start.'

'They'll be fine once the wind has got to them,' she said, 'but I can't stay and chat, I've got to "see a man about a dog"!'

'I hope that was merely an expression, and not something she intends to do,' said my aunt, with a peck on my cheek and a squeeze of my shoulder. And with that, the ladies left me to my thoughts, alone in my fiancé's apartment until Uncle Lawrence came for me.

Did I love Edward? Well... I was very fond of him, certainly, although after everything that happened it's hard to recall the good moments. He was tall, I'll give him that. Taller than me, even. And Edward had joked about the "impressive children" we would have so many times, I'd begun to wonder whether that was what this was all about.

I watched from the window, as Maude and my aunt got into the motorcar to head over to the church, stopping first to see the seamstress. They would then drive down Bloomsbury Street, turn onto Shaftesbury Avenue, and then past Fortnum & Mason's beautiful Christmas windows. How strange to be marrying on Christmas Eve, still, I was getting married, which was certainly something in this day and age. I would no longer be one of the "surplus women" the press enjoyed writing about. I would be married. I would have children. I would be happy.

Three

We were still a fair way from the church, when we heard the distant sound of the noonday peels of St James's, and my uncle examined his watch. I could only imagine how Reverend Parsley was managing, if Uncle Lawrence was anything to go by. A stickler for punctuality, he had moved into the front seat, next to the chauffeur, Baxter, when the lights had turned red, as they had done at almost every occasion between Belsize Park and Fitzrovia.

We finally reached St Xavier's, to find my aunt rushing down the steps – steps I should have been gliding up, at least half an hour earlier.

'Lawrence! Where on earth have you been?'

'We were involved in a minor altercation,' said my uncle, as he wrestled with the bride-side door. Sitting inside, I could tell it was badly scraped and dented, and the beautiful Bentley would be taking a little trip to the garage very soon.

Our driver, Baxter, began his service on the Godfrey family estate when they'd run a carriage rather than a motorcar – and the time it would take for the elderly chauffeur to get out, adjust his jacket, take off his cap, help to open the door, convey to me his best wishes, have a coughing fit, close the door, readjust his jacket, put his cap back on and get back into his seat, was time we could ill afford.

'Get her out the other side!' said Maude, who had followed my aunt down the church steps and, pushing my uncle aside, was yanking open the door. Urging me out, she fixed both men with her 'just-you-wait' face, as she took on bridesmaid duties, arranging my cloak hood, and smoothing the velvet, lace and silk.

I tried a smile, if only to calm everyone down. It failed. 'We were caught in traffic, and Baxter attempted a fancy manoeuvre which didn't quite come off,' I said. Where other trips to the church might have been spent waving back at well-wishers, chatting about the day to come and enjoying a snifter of brandy, ours had been spent exchanging words with a greengrocer about the state of his van.

As my uncle linked arms with me, and we began walking up the steps, my aunt overtook us at a sprint, ordering Maude to run with her and urging Lawrence to hurry up. We watched as they made it to the top step, slammed the impressive doors open and disappeared from view.

'Are you ready?' asked my uncle, as we reached the threshold, and peered into the candlelit church, which was festooned with winter greenery.

'I think so,' I said, taking a deep breath.

The congregation turned as we walked in, the music began, and those first few booming notes drowned out the sound of my aunt and her maid taking their seats. The first people I saw as we entered, were a couple on Edward's side of the aisle. The man had his head buried in a hymn book, but the woman was glowering and, judging by the black she was wearing, had been expecting a funeral. Strange, and under any other circumstances I would have let them know their mistake, but it was my wedding after all, in addition to which, after a quick look at his watch, my uncle had begun marching me down the aisle, double quick. He was making up for lost time, while the organist struggled to keep up with us.

Our side of the church was brimming with guests, and it included people I'd worked with, school friends, second-cousins, a couple of great-aunts and an uncle who'd brought his pet rabbit along. Bathsheba's three sons – my cousins – and their wives were doing their best to stop the children from playing with the pet, and they were joined by Margaret, my mother.

She had come over solo, leaving her man of the moment behind, which was just as well as far as Edward was concerned. (Learning that his mother-in-law's beau was a Mexican matador twenty years his junior had obviously left a sour taste in his mouth.) What was odder still, was that my matador-adoring mother was so keen on me getting married in the first place. I was born on the wrong side of the blanket and I guessed that my mother hoped that getting married would make things "right". Much as she loves penniless Marco, it helps that they live together in Mexico, rather than Monaco or Mayfair, but it is an oddly conventional attitude for her to take.

Seated next to her, were my aunt's writers who, with the exception of Jack, were a vision in creativity, colour and individuality. "A joy to behold", as my aunt would have said. Lettice, the Regency writer, tends towards lace and she did not disappoint. She was a vision in lavender. Bettina is rather less colourful, and I have no idea what she writes, although I gather that she's the principal reason that their books aren't readily available, and also the reason that they make any money at all. And what

Bettina's clothes lack in colour, they more than make up for in cut and quality, and this morning she was wearing cashmere, velvet and silk in an unusually cheery maroon.

And on Edward's side? Nanny was there of course, wearing some dreadfully gloomy outfit and a face to match. There was a small group of male friends; good, solid types who enjoy the fresh air, and who were polite enough not to openly stare at my lot on the other side. And then there was Edward standing, stock still, ramrod straight, an impressive figure of a man.

'Thirteen minutes past twelve o'clock exactly!' said my uncle, beaming at Edward who, as I was handed over, looked a little nonplussed, when he should of course have been gazing at me in adoration.

'You're supposed to GIVE her away, not throw her!' my aunt hissed as her husband took his seat, and then the man had the temerity to look down at his stopwatch, give it a tap and nod at Reverend Parsley. 'Time to get underway!' Fortunately, Parsley is a professionally forgiving man, and his usually benign expression had returned – that or he'd had a tot of something in the vestry, while he was waiting for us.

I also wished I'd thought to have a glass of sherry before the ceremony, but there we are; hindsight is a wonderful thing, and Jack must have thought the same, because I noticed her lean over and offer my aunt a nip from her flask.

'Dearly beloved, we are gathered here today, in the sight of God to join this man and this woman in holy matrimony...'

It was a pleasingly familiar service, odd as it felt for me to be at the centre of it. Reverend Parsley did a very good job, and the prayers were strangely moving. He wanted very much for this marriage to work – and so did I.

The prayers finished, we sang 'O God Our Help in Ages Past', and we got to the "if there be anyone present who" bit, at which point I stifled a nervous snigger, which was entirely silenced, when the odd couple at the back of the church stood up. They must have realised it wasn't a funeral, and they left with a loud slam of the door.

Without any further disturbances, we were announced to be husband and wife, we kissed, the organ was fired up, and Edward and I marched down the aisle, in a much more sedate fashion than my arrival.

After being showered with rice, I was surprised to see only one photographer present, and we waited a mere moment for photographs to be taken, before Edward announced he was hungry and said he was off to the reception with "Mrs M", and I was whisked down the steps by my new husband, to the waiting car.

I should explain; Weddings are my aunt's be-all-and-end-all. As I may have mentioned before, she runs a small publishing house, and weddings are wonderful publicity. All three of her son's marriages were covered by the national press gossip pages, with editorials written (by Bathsheba Godfrey) about how their love had been inspired by the many books of Kiss & Swoon, a series produced by the A Love Lost & Found Publishing House.

And this occasion was to have been no different, except that Edward hadn't managed to post a wedding notice in the Times, despite his many assurances. Aunt Bathsheba said she'd rung the papers to ensure their photographers would be there, but in the end only one had turned up. It was Edith Prendergast from Blooming Lovely, the horticulture magazine.

I gave the photographer a smile as I was bundled into the battered, black Bentley, holding my flowers as elegantly as I could. 'I hope you got a good shot,' I said, and Edith looked pleased, but I wasn't sure that my bouquet of ivy, roses and berries was quite impressive enough to be featured, given how badly squashed it had been in the incident with the green grocer's van.

Four

Seeing as Miss Prendergast had been good enough to turn up with her camera, I invited her to the reception that was being held in the Merchant's Hall, which was a wonderfully warm venue that had been beautifully decked out in holly, ivy and, of course, mistletoe. The Christmas tree next to the stairs in the foyer was generously decorated with red and gold baubles and a group of carol singers welcomed us in with a hearty rendition of *Ding Dong! Merrily on High*, which made me feel very festive – and I had to remind myself that Edward and I were here for a wedding, rather than a Christmas gathering.

While the guests milled about, finding their seats, I noticed one late arrival. He was an old army friend of Edward's who would have been best man if he'd arrived on time. If you can imagine a bulldog in human form, that was the man referred to as "Sarge". His jowls wobbled, his legs waddled, and he glared, glassy-eyed at everyone he met under glowering eyebrows.

'He's no oil painting, but he's certainly well-oiled,' said Jack, sucking at her pipe.

The military man tottered towards me and, steadying himself with a hand on a pillar, he twirled his moustache in a most unseemly manner. 'So, who are you?' he asked.

I pointed at my veil and when he still looked confused, I told him exactly who I was.

'Right. The bride. Right you are, well done. And you're the lucky fella?' he asked, turning to Jack. Before she could react, I tapped on the man's shoulder and pointed him in the direction of Edward, although I noticed that he promptly headed over to a group of ladies, who quickly dispersed.

After a lunch of roast beef with all the trimmings*, Edward made a speech, which was short and sweet and said everything that was required of it, and this was followed by his (interim) best man's speech, which was much shorter and not in the least bit sweet. It was, in fact, fairly practical in nature and I suspected the man had made a quick telephone call to his parents for some tips. (Never go upstairs without taking something up with you. Try not to argue before bedtime. Let the little lady be in charge of linen and crockery, while the man is in charge of the dogs and horses – that sort of thing.)

And after all that prudent advice, Sarge stood up and shouted a loud "CONGRATULATIONS TO CAP AND HIS MISSUS. HIP-HIP-HOO-" and stumbled back down to his seat.

My side of the family were getting antsy. In fact, the level of chat had risen considerably, even while Edward had been giving his speech. The writing ladies were smoking (much to Nanny's chagrin), my aunt was having an animated chat with an old friend of hers and my mother? She had begun dancing to the music that was drifting up from another party in the same building. Merrily twirling round the hall, she was wearing a bright appliqué cape she'd picked up in Monterrey. It was striking, certainly, but I wasn't sure about the naked couple embroidered on the back. Were they dancing? It was hard to tell.

'I never thought I'd see it happen, Georgie!' she called out as she twirled past me with a young waiter in her embrace.

'Have you actually spoken with the groom, Margaret?' my aunt asked. 'His name's Edward.'

'Yes! He introduced himself just before the hors d'oeuvres were served, and he said some very ordinary things about my outfit, but some surprisingly nice things about Georgie.' And she must have forgotten how close I was standing, when she then said, 'Although I'm not sure you're entirely sure about him, are you, Sheba?' I noticed my aunt pop a vol-au-vent in her mouth to avoid having to answer. It isn't polite to speak with one's mouth full.

Reaching for another passing waiter, my mother first took his bottle of champagne, and then his arm. 'And, did you know, Lawrie had the temerity to THANK me for not bringing Marco over!'

In an effort to rein in my mother's exuberance, I tapped my glass with a fork, stood up and told everyone it was time for cake. Sarge handed Edward a ceremonial sword and I stepped up and closed my hands over his. We cut the first few slices, a cheer went up, and the waiter took over, while I passed the plates around. It was, of course, fruit cake made by Cook, which had been liberally fed with brandy, coated in apricot jam, thick marzipan and a thin layer of icing, just the way I like it. Good for weddings and Christmas! (Well, really, any time of year...)

While the slices of cake circulated, I caught up with Edith, who was fiddling with her camera, and I congratulated her on her presence. 'It looks like your publication might be the only one with photographs!' I said gamely, trying to hide my disappointment. I had given my aunt a long list of all the photographers she could contact, it was the least I could do, given her generosity, and I knew she had sent the details out in good time.

'Yes, it's a bit of a scoop for us at Blooming Lovely, I must say. And a bit of luck too.'

'Why's that?'

'Well, I was chatting with Norbert Atkins –'

'The Marylebone Mercury?'

'That's the one, and he seemed to think that the wedding was being held at Saint Xenia's.'

'Saint Xenia?' I said, coughing into my champagne.

'I thought it unlikely. We're fairly up with all the churches, and that's a Russian Orthodox one, so I decided he'd got it wrong.'

'Why did he think it was being held there?'

'He said he'd received a call...'

I did my best to shield my concern by passing her a second chunk of cake, and taking another gulp of my drink. Who could have made that call, and why? Some enemy of the romantic publishing industry perhaps? I should have to look into it after the honeymoon, but for the moment it was time for more speeches, and it was my Uncle Lawrence's turn to take to the floor.

He began well enough, and then started telling stories from his own marriage – every one of which my aunt was forced to loudly deny. Finally, under her withering gaze, his speech began to wind down, although he finished well enough. 'I have two pieces of sage advice for the newly-weds. In order for a marriage to survive, one should always be punctual. And, at my own wedding, many moons ago, Bathsheba and I didn't leave as promptly as we should have done and, as a result, our honeymoon luggage was compromised. My new wife's underwear was replaced with that of my mother-in-law, and mine had been swapped with my nephew's, which made things distinctly awkward. Three cheers for the bride and groom!'

And as the hip-hip-hoorays died down, Edward took my arm and he suggested we leave.

The guests were fairly merry by this time – with red cheeks, shining eyes, and raised voices. And, a final measure intended to keep everyone occupied was Edward singing a couple of lines of "The Twelve Days of Christmas" as we left the room, and from then on, the wedding reception became a Christmas party. My aunt, however, was not to be fooled. She followed me and Edward, catching up with us as we bumped into Sarge, my new husband's old army chum.

'I can see you!' he roared. 'Trying to get out without anyone noticing!'

'Shhh, old boy!' said Edward with a grin. 'Just trying to get out without too much fuss.'

'Come on, Cap, fuss is what it's all about,' said the man, giving me a wink. 'Just ask the little missus here. Though I'm sure she'll take charge if you step out of line, eh!'

'Go back inside, King. Make the most of the bottle of Glen Grant behind the bar,' said Edward.

'That's not a bad shout!' The ruddy-faced man, had clearly made a sizable dent in several bottles of whatever was available already, but his tone when he next spoke, was almost prim. 'I've joined a tasting club, don't you know, so I'm a bit of an expert when it comes to the "water of life", and a bottle of Glen Grant would be a form of study, if you will... Where you off to, anyway?' he asked.

'None of your b-'

'Come on, Cap! You can't pull the wool over my eyes,' he said, tapping his nose, and letting out a loud hiccup. 'Reckon I know, anyway. Now, I really ought to leave you good people alone, and make friends with a life-giving bottle of GG.' He tottered back to the reception and, while my aunt helped me with my veil, my husband called me a cab.

'But I thought you were going together, Edward?' said my aunt, something I'd thought too.

'We are, we are, but I'll take the car, while wifey pops back to the apartment and gets changed.' He turned to me. 'I'll meet you out the front of the apartment in an hour's time. I've just got something I have to do. See you shortly.' He must have seen the look on my aunt's face, because he took her hand, gave it a kiss and thanked her for the charming reception.

Edward helped me into the cab, but it wasn't the departure I'd had in mind, and I could tell that my aunt felt the same way, as she opened the door and got in with me, saying she would help me with my dress. And I was about to close the door, when Maude jumped in beside us, and gave the cabby the address. Edward banged on the roof, and we were off – and swiftly overtaken by Jack on her motorcycle.

*Gravy, roast potatoes, carrots, Savoy cabbage with butter and black pepper, Yorkshire puddings, horseradish sauce and English mustard.

Five

My honeymoon case was packed, of course, and expectantly sitting on the bed where I'd left it. We wrestled with my veil, Maude undid the hundred-and-one pretty, little buttons, and then she helped me to take off my wedding dress, and we all enjoyed the last of the brandy and wished each other a Happy Christmas. Finally, dressed in my going-away outfit (an exquisite red-wool Paquin suit, care of my cousin's wife), I reapplied my lipstick while Maude examined the state of my dress, covered it in a sheet and hung it up. We left the tiara in its box on the dressing table.

'How do I look?' I asked.

'Edward's a very lucky man,' said my aunt. 'You look stunning.'

Maude obviously didn't agree, because she began interfering with my hair, and after a testy five minutes, my short curls were rearranged and my hat was firmly secured on my head by a scarf, all the better to survive the drive.

Jack had followed us to the apartment on her motorcycle, but when she dismounted, she'd gone off to talk to the char lady, which was no help to us at all. And so, I was left to lug my luggage to the lift, insisting (quite rightly) that I was the strongest of the three of us.

'And I suppose your new husband has his case in the car?' said Maude.

'Oh no,' I said. 'He left it with the doorman.'

'Well, when did he manage that?' she asked, and I was as perplexed as the rest of them – and then just as relieved, when the lift doors opened, and the doorman offered me his congratulations, and helped me with my case.

Clouds had gathered since we'd arrived, and a beautiful but frosty day had turned into an afternoon heavy with the promise of a flurry. There was snow on the way and a certain cold city stillness and quiet, that was suddenly broken by Jack's voice from behind us. She was inside the foyer, with her head sticking out between the entrance doors, and she was obviously up to something.

'Georgie! About your wedding present,' she said. 'I know you'll like it, but I just want you to agree that you'll like it before I give it to you.'

'I'm sure I'll like whatever it is,' I said, although I could see that my aunt wasn't convinced.

'Good. Close your eyes, and hold out your hands.'

'Close my eyes?'

'It'll make it more exciting,' said Jack.

'Righto!' I said, doing my best to drum up an enthusiasm I didn't feel, and which was further tempered when Jack told my aunt and Maude that they had to close their eyes too.

They duly did so, if only to find out the answer to this mystery gift. I know that my aunt had given Jack strict instructions not to give us fish knives, even as a joke, but I wasn't sure they would merit this kind of fuss.

And that was when I heard a curious skittering sound and a whimper, and I felt something, warm, soft and wriggly in my hands. I shrieked, and when I opened my eyes, it was to see a small dog in my arms. Not a puppy, but certainly juvenile – and certainly not a conventional hunting dog. Some kind of wire-haired terrier. An absolute darling. I struggled with the little creature, which was doing its best to lick off my lipstick.

'Her name's Crumpet,' said Jack. 'I won her in a game yesterday, and I immediately thought of you.'

'If you had bought them fish knives, Jacqueline,' said my aunt, 'They could have been stored in the bottom drawer of that kitchen and never spoken of again. But a dog!' The little thing gave out a high-pitched yip and carried on its enthusiastic licking.

'She is a proper present,' said Jack, 'And you're only sore because I didn't get a couple of Persian cats!'

'Altogether a much more sensible pet, although Crumble certainly seems to have taken to you,' she said with a sigh.

'And what are your plans for tonight, aunt?' I asked, eager to change the subject.

'We shall go back to the wedding reception to pick up your mother, and when we've had a bite of supper, we shall return to Saint Xavier's for Carols, mince pies and mulled wine, before popping back to Ampney Tet for the night. You know how your uncle likes to wake up in the ancestral home on Christmas morning and – don't make that face, Maude! And besides, at Christmas we call a truce on discussions regarding Tet's future, so it's rather relaxing. No mention of the sale of paintings, the demolition of the east wing – or the letting go of staff.' She raised her eyebrows at Maude, who took no notice at all.

It began to snow, and in the five minutes we had been waiting outside, the trees around us were laced with a delicate layer of snowflakes, and the blank, white sky promised more.

'And you'll drive Mummy down to Southampton tomorrow?' I asked.

'Lawrence will, yes. I believe her boat sails at three.'

We all shivered as the wind picked up, and my eyes were stung by a sudden flurry of snow. 'Didn't she say it was cheaper to sail on Christmas Day?'

'Yes, something like that,' said my aunt, nodding, and we continued to stand in the cold, huddling together for warmth.

(Where on earth was Edward? He was ten minutes late. What was he up to? And wasn't it the bride's prerogative to be tardy, not the groom's?)

The dog suddenly began furiously barking and, as I struggled to control the furry, little ball of energy, we heard the sound of tyres, and turned to see the approach of Edward's Sunbeam.

'Well, Crumpet, I don't know where we're going,' I said, 'But we're off on our honeymoon, and wherever it is it's bound to be warmer than this.'

The Sunbeam stopped, and Edward got out, looking every bit as smart as he had at the church. 'Hello all! Had to give the car a once-over, because the steering was a bit iffy,' he said, 'But it's all fixed now.' He patted the car's bonnet, and suddenly noticed the little dog in my arms.

'What –'

'Look, darling, a present!' I said, 'Isn't she lovely?' But my joy was not mirrored by the expression on my husband's face.

'She's fully trained,' said Jack, 'Well – mostly trained, if you know what I mean. Your char lady has looked after Crumpet all of today, and said there was only one little accident. She wasn't any trouble at all.'

With his beady eyes fixed on the "gift" in my arms, Edward picked up my case and retrieved his own, and when he'd loaded them into the boot, he dutifully wished my aunt a "Happy Christmas". His goodbye wishes to Jack weren't quite as effusive, and his reaction to the small wiry-haired animal he found sitting on the driver's seat wasn't at all favourable. They regarded each other warily and after a growling stand-off, Crumpet jumped into the back seat. I was sure it would be fine, they just needed some time together.

Six

Edward and I were married – how exciting! And we were off on our honeymoon, although I had no idea where to. 'Oh darling, can't you at least, give me a clue?' I asked, as we edged into the London traffic.

'Somewhere very special. It's going to be a surprise.'

'How exciting. And the ceremony was lovely, wasn't it, Edward?'

'Yes, yes it was,' he said, and he grinned, but his expression suddenly changed as he looked beyond me — and then jammed on the brakes and swerved to avoid a van that had stopped in front of us.

'But, who were those people on your side?' I asked.

'Huh?'

'That couple at the back of the church.'

'I don't know who you're talking about, dear,' he said.

'There was a woman at the back of the church, Edward. Wearing black, and sitting with a man. I assumed that she'd arrived for a funeral and got the time wrong, but she got up and left when –'

'I've no idea, Georgiana,' he said. 'Obviously a mistake, anyway, it doesn't matter. We're married now, Mrs M, and we're off for some time alone. Just the two of us.'

'I'm so looking forward to a week in... where are we going again?'

'Ha! You won't catch me like that!' he said, although I could have sworn that we were moving westwards, and very much NOT in the direction of the Côte d'Azur. It had been a long, wet summer, a dismal autumn, and a week away in the sun, or warmer climes at least, was something I had been looking forward to ever since Edward had proposed. And it was with that in mind that I'd packed my emerald silk beach pyjamas – just in case. They were a gift from one of my cousin's wives, and they were simply dreamy, and I closed my eyes for a moment, and tried to imagine the sun on my face and warm sand beneath my toes, but the illusion was spoiled by my shivering.

I wasn't sure that the temperature inside the car was any better than outside, and I wrapped my aunt's cloak around my knees.

Two hours after we'd left London, I had resigned myself to the fact that we would not be spending our wedding night drinking champagne and nibbling mussels, and I had been rather grateful when the little dog had sidled into the front and made a nest on my lap. I had also swapped my velvet cloche, for a woollen beret. It wasn't the going-away outfit I'd had in mind, but I had to admit that late December wasn't the ideal time for a honeymoon.

'The reception was nice, wasn't it?' I said, scrunching up my eyes, and trying to see where we were going through the sleet.

'Nice enough!' said Edward, 'And speaking of which, who was that fellow you were dancing with before I cut the cake? The one with the striped trousers?'

'Striped trousers? Oh, that was Julian.'

'Another cousin of yours?'

'I'm fairly sure I've introduced you to all of them, and no, he works at Domestic Bliss. He writes half the articles and all the titles, while it's my job to make sure we look good on the newsstand. I'm the one who chooses the best photographs, the right font in a nice, bright colour, and interesting illustrations. If we don't have a really eye-catching cover, people will buy The Queen magazine or The Lady, when they should be buying us.'

'Us?' Edward grinned as he said it, and I tried to smile back, but the truth was I would miss my work on the magazine and, despite its name, once a member of staff at the magazine had found actual "domestic bliss", they were expected to leave. Married ladies couldn't write for married ladies. Besides which, I had the distinct feeling that Edward would have asked me to leave, if I hadn't left of my own accord.

'Anyway, Julian is good fun,' I said, 'And he won't be losing his job any time soon.'

'The men don't have to leave when they tie the knot?'

'That, and I'm not sure that Julian is the tying-the-knot type.'

'Oh, yes?' said Edward. 'Man about town, eh?'

'Something like that,' I said. 'Sarge was interesting...'

'Been with me a long time. Bit of a mess at the reception though.'

'Hm, he was a bit squiffy.'

'I found him behind the bar, sleeping off that bottle of whiskey. Cradling it in his arms like a baby!'

'When I saw him, he was awake and upright!'

'Yes, I popped back to the reception to check on him, while you were getting changed with the ladies, and – oh – there's a pub!'

'Oh goody, let's stop and warm up a bit. We've been going for ages.'

The King's Head was just outside Aylesbury. The tinsel-decorated wireless was playing Christmas Carols, and there were a couple of chairs free, next to a roaring fire. Edward left Crumpet in the car, and ordered for both of us, while the dog barked outside.

'You can bring the little mite in,' said the landlady. 'It's awful cold.'

'Terriers are perfectly able to manage in this,' said Edward, ignoring the look on the lady's face.

'She has a point,' I said. 'Shouldn't we bring Crumpet in? It is freezing out there.'

'Silly idea for a wedding present if you ask me,' he said. 'The dog will be fine, and ah – here are our drinks!'

We were brought mulled cider and sausage rolls, which was just what the doctor ordered.

'Married at last!' said Edward taking a sip, and he gave his hot drink a thoughtful stir with its cinnamon stick. 'What IS that curious smell?'

'Sorry, I think it's my aunt's opera cape warming up. The fur's quite old.'

'She could have bought you something a bit more up-to-date for your wedding,' he said. 'I noticed she didn't stint on her own outfit.'

'Let's not talk about money, Edward. Not now.'

'I'm just not sure that an aging cape that's making a smell like that, is quite the thing. And I think it's a bit singed...'

I managed to snatch it away before it caught, but the damage was done. It would not grace the Theatre Royal or the Adelphi again, but it might just keep me alive. I glanced out of the window and noticed that the light was beginning to fade, and the weather had taken an even nastier turn. I had managed to catch sight of the map in Edward's pocket, and I had to assume that we were on our way to the Cotswolds – a very scenic part of the country that was, nevertheless, the region in which I had grown up. It was an area that was entirely familiar and entirely un-riviera, and home to my aunt and uncle's country estate.

With a spicy warmth in our bellies, we headed out to a cold car and a very cross little dog.

An hour or so later, darkness had descended, and Edward told me that we were all of ten minutes away from "home". We drove up and down lanes, taking multiple right and left-hand turns, and yet wherever we went, it felt like we were being followed. Edward had slowed, and sped up to allow for tight corners, and passing cars, but still the light behind us kept pace with us. Nothing unusual about that, you may say – there were few places to overtake on these narrow, winding country lanes, but I asked Edward to stop the car for a moment, to readjust one of the windscreen wipers that was sticking, because the heavy sleet had turned to wet snow. Edward stopped in a lay-by, and while he saw to the wiper, I gave Crumpet half of the sausage roll that I'd saved, and glanced behind us, out of the back window of the car. I could still see the single light, which had stopped still, when it should surely have overtaken us. It was no night to be out, riding a motorcycle and, just for a moment, I wondered whether Jack wanted her dog back – but I know the sound of her machine and this was much deeper. Edward jumped back in the car, letting in another flood of cold air. 'All done and off we go.'

'And I hope that wherever we're going is half as nice as the King's Head,' I said. 'A roaring fire, a big pot of stew, a glass of claret and a pile of hot minced pies!' I decided to ignore Edward's silence. It wasn't a good sign, but perhaps he hadn't heard me for the rush of wind.

He started up the car and within a minute, I thought, perhaps that single light was gone, although with the weather as it was, it was hard to tell.

We passed through a little village called Mean Withering, up a lane, down a lane, round a corner, down another lane and Edward finally stopped at a little cottage. Even in the gloom, it was beautiful. Small but friendly windows peered out from under a protective thatched roof that was covered in snow and beginning to blot out the gate's holly and ivy wreath.

'Oh, Edward, how lovely!'

'Actually, it's the one next door we're staying in,' he said, gazing fondly at the next cottage along.

There was no welcome shining from this household, no sign of habitation or warmth, no wreath, no twinkling lights and even the thatch wasn't quite as thick or luxuriant.

Edward wrestled with the key, and then wrestled with the door, which didn't want to open. And when the cottage did eventually let us in, a part of me wished it hadn't. This was our Christmas honeymoon getaway?

Seven

When Edward had announced a Christmas wedding, I'd suggested a week in the south of France, but he'd had his own plans, saying only that we were going somewhere he wanted me to see. His birthright. This drab little home might have been part of his family lore, but I would have preferred almost any other cottage in the Cotswolds, or, indeed, a week with my (new) husband, in his (new) place in town.

Edward's flat in Belsize Park was on the City and South London Railway line, only four tube stops from the British Museum. For the month before the wedding, Edward had given up his glorious, modern, warm apartment, and allowed me and Jack to live there, and we had loved every minute of its plush carpets and shiny chrome radiators. But this cottage was freezing cold; I took off my beret, scarf and cape, determined to "feel the benefit" now that I was indoors.

'I know you fancy yourself a city slicker, but this'll be just the ticket,' said Edward, putting our cases down.

'I love the Cotswolds, it just isn't what I was expecting,' I said, looking at the layer of dust on the table, and wondering what Maude would have made of it.

Edward took me in his arms, and warmed me up for a moment. 'I shall get the fire going, and take the cases up, Mrs M, if you fetch that dog and the hamper from the back of the car.'

'A cup of tea would be wonderful!'

'Oh, and we don't have any milk... perhaps you could try next door and if you can't get any from them, there will be milk at the inn.'

'There's an inn?'

'A pub on the corner. We passed it on the way down. It's just at the end of the lane.'

The quicker I fetched some milk, and got Crumpet and the basket of food inside, the quicker I could close the door, make a pot of tea and feel the life return to my fingers – they were still jangling with the cold. I put my cape back on, and my half-frozen beret, I stepped outside, and a sudden gust of snow almost blew me off my feet. I gently closed the front door behind me and knocked on the neighbouring door, but there was no answer.

I trudged over to the car. My hands were shaking so much from the cold, it took me a while to get the key into the lock and, given that we were in the Cotswolds, why on earth had Edward bothered to lock it – especially with Crumpet inside? The little dog jumped out and began barking wildly. She ran up the pitch-black lane, away from the cottage, and I reluctantly ran after her up and down, back and forth in the cold and driving snow. By the time I finally caught up with her, my coat was stiff with chunks of ice, I had laddered my stockings on a holly bush (very festive) and I had shouted something very unbecoming of a married woman on Christmas Eve.

And suddenly, a pub appeared out of nowhere – The Green Man – a beacon of beery light in the snowy darkness. I heard a roar of joyful, raised voices (in contrast with my own) and I wondered how warm it was inside. I could feel the cold of the snow that had melted through the seams of my cape, my jacket, my cardigan and blouse, and I thought back to my wedding reception and the beautifully dry dress I'd been wearing. Crumpet was scratching at the saloon door, and I pounced on her and fixed her lead to her collar.

'No more games! If you ever do that again, there will be hell to pay! My shoes are soaked, and I just know they'll go hard when they dry, and if that's the case I will not be held responsible for my actions. I could –' I growled at her, when I realised that the door was being held open by the landlord, who had obviously heard the sound of scratching – and everything I'd said too.

I entered, squeaking with every snowy step and, with Crumpet in tow, I demanded milk.

The expression on the landlord's face was one of surprise, and I realised that the expression on mine was still angry, and not the right one at all for someone asking for a pint of milk at a drinking establishment on Christmas Eve.

I wiped my eyes. 'I'm sorry, I'll start again. My husband – you see, the dog ran off, I've laddered my silk stockings... I'm feeling rather cold and frankly murderous. This is not the Christmas, or the honeymoon, I had in mind. You aren't speaking French or serving champagne, and I'm not staying in a chic little hôtel in St Tropez.' I took a deep breath, 'I would be very grateful if you had a bottle of milk to spare. I do have money.'

I realised that my "start again" wasn't as polite as I'd planned, but the landlord nodded his head, wished me a Happy Christmas and said he would see what they had. After firmly telling one of the regulars to be quiet – that he would have his pint of stout in a minute – the landlord went back behind the bar, in search of his wife.

I stood with the dog, warming my hands at the fire while the locals regarded me; a grumpy lady from the city who'd marched in with demands. The bar had quietened considerably since I'd arrived, except for the loud man in search of a drink, who had started suggesting that I might like a pint of stout too. I was relieved to hear an older man call out, 'Pipe down, Bill! She've already said she's on 'er unnymoon, and it's 'igh time you went 'ome!' I chatted with Crumpet and kept myself to myself.

The landlord returned with his wife, who gave me half a pint of milk to tide me over, and informed me that The Green Man was very welcoming on Christmas Day, so I thanked her with as warm a smile as I could muster, and said I would probably see them soon. I braced myself before I opened the door and headed back out into the cold.

Crumpet and I trudged back down the long lane in silence; the snow was falling more heavily now. I scrabbled with the car key and managed to get the Fortnum & Mason's hamper out (which was jolly nice), and I slammed the boot shut and turned to the cottage door. I pushed at it, but it had properly shut again, so I knocked and then called for Edward, but the weather was so wild, I wasn't sure he could hear me. My mood sunk again, and so, with the dog's lead between my teeth and the hamper in one hand, and the key and the milk in the other, I barged against the door and fell into the still dark, still cold cottage.

'Call yourself a country boy, Edward? The fire isn't up to much...' I muttered. 'It needs much more wood, and it does need to be PROPERLY LIT. And I may not be wonderfully house-proud, but you've left the place in a heck of a mess in the short time I've been – Edward! Where are you?'

I heard sounds from upstairs, and so did Crumpet, who'd begun whining.

'Oh no you don't,' I said. 'I'm not having your muddy paw-prints all over my honeymoon bed, and you can stop making that racket! You're staying here.' I tied the little dog to the banister and trooped into the kitchen with the hamper. The room was bleak and not what I was expecting, but it was, at least, clean, although all the cupboard doors and drawers had been left open. I filled the kettle, and hung it from the hook above the fire, which I added a couple of pieces of wood to and, when I was sure that they were burning, I spent a moment warming my hands.

'I got us the milk you asked for,' I called up. 'And the landlady at The Green Man says they're open tomorrow. The hamper's lovely, but I don't want to spend all day trying to work the oven, although I should look at what's in the basket before I...'. I couldn't make out his answer from upstairs, so when I was sure my fingers were alive, I went up to see the rest of the cottage, and help Edward unpack the cases.

There were a couple of rooms upstairs, but no light, and the wind howled through a rickety window, and it felt colder up here than it had downstairs. On one side was a small bedroom, with a neat little bed and a cot, its bareness illuminated by the moon, and the other door was shut, with my suitcase outside it on the landing. There was the sound of banging and I called out, 'Hoy – Edward! What are you doing? Whatever it is, I hope you're not building a bed or something!' No answer. I pushed the door, but it wouldn't open.

'Edward?' I tried the ice-cold door handle again. 'Edward? Where are you?' No answer. 'Come on, it's too cold, this is no time for jokes,' but as I said the words, I felt a small part of myself cringe. I could feel in my bones that now was not a time for jokes at all, and I pushed at the door again, harder. It still wouldn't budge, and there was still no answer.

Eight

The silence was heavy. 'Edward, are you all right?'

Crumpet joined me on the landing outside the bedroom, and began scratching at the floor and whining.

'Oh, Crumpet, how did you untie yourself?' I asked, shivering. 'Come on, little dog. I think, we need to get some help.'

I tried the cottage next door, but they still weren't home. They must have gone to church for a Christmas service, or perhaps they were delivering presents. That's what people do at Christmas, isn't it? Not disappear, or lock themselves in a room. Or stay silent.

We skidded up the lane, snow squeaking underfoot. There wasn't a soul about all the way up to The Green Man, and it was only as we reached the pub and stopped, that I allowed my fear to overcome me and I hesitated at the saloon door. The little dog's bark urged me inside.

'Back so soon?' asked the landlord.

'She couldn't keep away!' said one of the drinkers – it was the man who'd made such a fuss earlier.

'I'm having trouble with a door. My fiancé is behind it, and he's not saying anything.' I looked around and nobody moved, so I tried again. 'Can someone help me to open it, please? It's my husband –'

'Make your mind up, you married, engaged or what?' said the drunkard, with a leer that I did not like the look of.

'Come now, Bill, no need for that,' said the landlord. 'The lady needs help.' He poked the shoulder of a tall, young lad leaning on the bar, saying 'Go on, Rod. You're big enough to shift anything. Off you go.'

The young man obediently left his post, opened the saloon door for me, and the two of us walked along in the dark.

'So, you're stayin' down 'ere, are you? We don't of'en see strangers in this neck of the woods.'

Truthfully, I wasn't in the mood to chat, but social convention demanded that small talk be made, so I told him it was a beautiful part of the country – which it is – and I introduced myself. The young man confirmed that his name was Rodney, and said, 'Forriners usually stay in one of them fancier villages.' I wasn't about to tell him that I'd grown up twenty miles away but then, perhaps that was his definition of a foreigner. We arrived at the cottage, and Rodney knocked the snow off his boots and managed to open the front door with ease. 'I'm assumin' that ain't the one that's stuck?' he said.

'No, it's the bedroom door,' I replied, and where I might have expected a smirk from one of his drinking companions, Rodney nodded and followed me up the stairs.

He turned the handle, and after using a bit more force – and failing, the lad took a step back, and barged shoulder-first into the door, which burst open, with a flurry of snow. The window was up and the shutters banged open, closed and open again, and with an icy gust the window suddenly slammed shut and its glass cracked – but held.

'There we are, Mrs Mortimer,' he said. 'No prob-'

The word sat unfinished on his tongue, because there was a problem. Edward was lying on the floor with a sword in his heart. A sword that I had last seen slicing through our wedding cake.

Rodney took a step forward, and I yelled, 'Don't touch him!' and then realised that the young man was swaying, and he sagged to the floor, in a faint.

Trying not to look at the blade sticking out of Edward's chest, I patted Rodney until he came round. He looked like he was going to be sick, and the dog's whines had turned to howls.

When Rodney was able to get to his feet, I bundled him into the hallway, closed the door, and ran downstairs to take the whistling kettle off the fire. When the lad had made it down the stairs, I wrapped him in my aunt's opera cape and told him to sit down while I made him a cup of sweet tea. He looked very pale, and not all there. Waiting for the kettle to come back to the boil, I drifted off for a moment, away from the awful reality I faced.

I tried to imagine the Christmas I might have had. Mince pies and mulled wine at St Xavier's with my aunt and uncle, while my mother regaled everyone with a Spanish Carol or two – she has the most marvellous voice. And then they would drive across the country, to Ampney Tet, my Uncle Lawrence's pride and joy. The house is old, and cold, and they would awaken to see their breath, but the view would more than make up for it.

My dreams of pastural beauty were pierced by a shrill scream, as the kettle came to the boil. I made Rodney a cup of tea and, when he'd taken a couple of sips, I instructed him to hold the dog's lead, while I headed out doors, alone and shivering, back to The Green Man, through the driving snow.

I don't remember saying anything when I opened the door, but it turned out that the local copper was one of the men drinking at the bar and when he saw me arrive alone, he got up and immediately left with me.

We returned to the cottage and I recall pointing to him to go upstairs, while I stayed downstairs with Crumpet, and Rodney staggered back to the pub to call for reinforcements.

I made a fresh pot of tea and asked if I could help but, of course, there was nothing to be done.

Nine

Christmas day was an odd one. I cried and drank tea, and then cried some more and drank some more tea.

Edward was still upstairs, and he remained there until the local physician was located, and brought to the cottage. The doctor had spent Christmas Eve at a barge party in Inglesham, and it was only when the lockkeepers were asked to keep an eye out for the Yellow Rose, that Dr Charters was found at all. He arrived with his bag (which was surely unnecessary) and a smudge of lipstick on his cheek, and when he announced that the man upstairs with the sword in his chest was indeed dead, I began to shake and giggle. It had already been a very long day, and it was only half past seven in the morning.

While I nibbled on a lump of Stilton from the hamper, gazing into the fire, I imagined my mother, my aunt and uncle, enjoying devilled kidneys, bacon and kippers in Ampney Tet's morning room. They were all of twenty miles away but it might as well have been a thousand. They were living in a world where Edward and I were still married, unaware that our honeymoon was well and truly over.

My mother would sail back to Marco in Mexico today, and Aunt Bathsheba and Maude would return to the warmth of the

Pimlico townhouse, while my uncle stayed on at the estate, or perhaps headed to his club, for a little peace and quiet.

The doctor quietly cleared his throat, and Crumpet and I joined him in the kitchen for a medicinal ginger wine, courtesy of The Green Man, while two young constables carried Edward out on a stretcher. When he'd finished his glass, the doctor went outside to talk with the ambulance driver, and I realised how heavily it was snowing when he returned indoors, brushing the snow from his coat. 'Your case will be brought down, momentarily, although it might be just as well if you stayed downstairs. I see it's comfortable enough. Now, would you mind telling me when you last saw your husband alive?'

I hoped Dr Charters didn't see the puzzled look on my face, until I remembered that I was married, and that the husband he was talking about was mine. My wedding night just hadn't been what I was expecting. I explained my confusion – that we had just arrived, and that Edward and I had been married in the afternoon.

'Christmas Eve?' he said. 'Very romantic.'

'Yes, we thought so.' The two of us stood in silence for a moment, as we realised how unfortunate it all was.

'The constable here will stay for a few more hours – until his lunch, I should think – or until Detective Inspector Routledge arrives, whichever of those things happens first. Oh, and I meant to say, when I passed the pub earlier, the landlady made it clear that if you would like to spend the day at The Green Man, in their parlour, you would be most welcome. They are a rum lot, but quite well behaved, generally.'

I thanked him for the offer, but couldn't imagine that I was quite what the regulars had in mind for their Christmas Day knees-up.

'Crummy and I will be fine, thank you.'

'I'm sorry?' he asked.

'My dog, Crumpet.'

'Right, I see,' he said, looking down at the little terrier, who was sniffing his medical bag. Dr Charters snatched at the handles, and Crumpet took a step back and bared her teeth.

'Well, I am sorry for your loss, Mrs Mortimer. Good day to you – and a Happy – good day to you.' Stumbling over his words, the doctor quickly tipped his hat and I was left standing on the doorstep, looking out at the beautiful, blinding white landscape.

Mrs Mortimer.

"Mrs Mortimer".

Mrs Georgiana Mortimer.

I had written my new signature so many times over the last month, on the back of envelopes and receipts, that it was second nature to me, but I wasn't sure it counted now, did it, without Edward by my side? I felt sad and a little silly, to be honest. I had married a man I barely knew, and been taken away to a part of the country I knew far too well, to stay in a mysterious "honeymoon" location.

My mind was whirling; what would my aunt say? What would everyone say? My husband (could I call him that?) had been murdered (although nobody had mentioned the 'm' word yet) and all I had to show for our marriage was a dog, a car and a hamper. And the police were treating me like I was the last person to see Edward alive, when that obviously wasn't the case at all.

I shivered, although I don't know why; the fire was roaring, and having spent too many hours huddled in front of it, I was half-cooked, when I got up to let Crumpet out for a sniff of a tree.

A couple of hours later, there was a knock at the door. It was the landlady, who arrived with a roast turkey lunch, and a bag of mince pies. It was kind of her to be so... kind, but noticeable that she didn't enter the house, and that she told me not to worry about returning the plate. Crumpet and I shared the roast by the fireside – a late breakfast, or an early elevenses – after which I did some tidying up. The cottage had been left in a terrible state the night before, and I had nothing better to do. I put the kettle on and, by the time the pot had brewed, the ground floor was looking respectable. I drank my tea while nibbling at a mince pie, curled up in the armchair in front of the fire, with the dog on my lap.

I had been told to stay where I was until the inspector arrived, and the constable had said that his boss would be round before lunch, so I stretched, washed with cold water, and had another cup of tea, while Crumpet had the quails' eggs from the hamper. (It wasn't until later that I realised what a bad idea that was for a small dog's tummy.) We must have been dozing when the constable left for Christmas Day with his family, because I don't recall saying goodbye to him – or Crumpet barking.

And so, the two of us were stuck in a dilapidated cottage in the middle of the Cotswolds, in the middle of winter; sitting together was warmer than sitting apart, and sharing a meal was easier than making two. I was little Crummy's family now, just as she was mine, but this was not the domestic bliss I had signed up for.

Ten

The loud knock on the door sent me and Crumpet flying from the comfort of our armchair. Trying to recover from our rude awakening, I straightened my skirt, arranged my hair and opened my eyes wide as I reached for the latch and readied myself for a blast of cold air. Standing outside, was a middle-aged man, of middling height, with sandy brown hair, grey eyes and an intense stare – and I realised that while I'd been sizing him up, he had been doing the same to me.

'Mrs Mortimer, I presume?'

'Yes, good afternoon, officer.'

'Detective Inspector Routledge, Woodstock Station. May I?'

The inspector stamped the snow from his shoes, and tipped his bowler hat, but didn't take it off as he walked in, and I didn't blame him. The cottage still felt icy, and whenever I wasn't directly in front of the hearth, I had been using Crumpet for warmth.

Routledge stood in the middle of the room, silently summing up the cottage, its contents and Crumpet, until I offered him a cup of tea.

'Thank you, yes,' he said. 'And my condolences on your husband's passing.'

'Yes, I found him –'

'– I was given to understand that it was Mr Rodney Collingwood who found the body, the constable's younger brother.'

'No, I, well, yes, I suppose he was the one who broke the door in, so strictly speaking-'

'He was the one who found the body, and I spoke with him at length, after he'd returned from the Christmas morning service.'

Why was I beginning to feel guilty about the fact that my husband had been murdered at Christmas? It wasn't my fault! But as I stood there, I began to get the horrible feeling that they may feel that it was my fault. That I had murdered Edward. I turned to the kettle as it began to whistle and, without thinking, I picked it up with a wet cloth – the heat seared my skin and I let the kettle go, dropping it back onto the hook it hung on, steaming water splashing over my legs.

'Dammit!' And then I burst into tears. Shame, pain, anger, shock and fear coursed down my cheeks, but where was the grief? I wiped my eyes and realised that my sudden outburst had knocked the inspector off his perch. He'd stopped peering at the cottage, and walked to the window to look at the snow outside.

When my burnt hand had stopped throbbing, I made the inspector his cup of tea (milk, no sugar), and offered him a piece of wedding cake, which Maude had been kind enough to add to my case.

He took the cup, and declined the offer of an early afternoon nibble. The cake had been well fed, and if he was "on duty" and not drinking, it probably wasn't entirely suitable. I put the plate down, but snatched it back up when Crumpet gave it a sniff.

'I was led to believe that the cottage was in a state of some disarray, Mrs Mortimer, and you were unable to determine whether it was your husband or someone else who had caused it,' he said.

'That is correct,' I replied, and I ignored the look on the inspector's face when I told him that I'd tidied up just before he'd arrived.

'Can you tell me more about your relationship with your husband?'

'Edward –'

He read his notes. 'Yes. Edward Arthur St. John Mortimer?'

'He and I were married yesterday afternoon.'

'Christmas Eve,' he said. 'Known each other long, Mrs Mortimer?'

'No. Not very long. Three months.'

'Rather hasty?'

'Yes, well. He wanted to, he sort-of insisted. I was happy to wait, but he said he couldn't.'

'Was there a reason for that?'

'Because he wanted to. He wanted to marry me, and... well, Edward is – he was – older than me.'

'I see,' he said. (What did the inspector see?) 'And would you go over the events of last night for me?'

'But I've already told Constable Collingwood.'

'His notes were not comprehensive. If you would go over them again, I'd be most grateful.'

So, I told him about our arrival and that Edward hadn't brought any milk. I told him the cottage wasn't what I'd been expecting and when I mentioned the south of France, he put me back on course.

The inspector was more interested when I told him about the sounds in the room above, less interested when he realised that I hadn't really heard anything, and even less interested when I told him that I thought we'd been followed some of the way to Mean Withering. 'Everyone feels like that around here, he said. It's the price they pay for these ridiculous roads.'

'You're not a local, then?'

'Do I sound like a local?' the inspector asked, and when he began to complain about rural postings and the quiet of the country, it was my turn to get him back on track. He was, after all, investigating my husband's murder.

'Before I go upstairs, I understand from Collingwood's notes, that the weapon used was the same one that you used to cut your wedding cake?'

I put my plate down, and the inspector went upstairs.

Listening to Detective Inspector Routledge walking about in the bedroom above me, I cast my mind back to the night before, and what I had heard then. Of course, I hadn't expected Edward to be up there with someone, fighting for his life, so I hadn't given any thought to what I was hearing. And thinking back now, how did the sounds differ? It was less noisy now, but – oh, what was the point? There must have been two of them upstairs, he hadn't stabbed himself with the ceremonial sword, after all. Although, it was an odd thing for my new husband to have brought with him. I didn't recall seeing the sword in the car, but then remembered that Edward had said that he had popped back to the reception to check on Sarge. Perhaps he'd picked it up then – and I wondered what else he'd done.

Whoever the murderer was, they'd left from the window, and escaped in the snow, which had been falling too hard to leave any footprints behind. And it was falling hard now, too.

The inspector returned downstairs. 'Thank you for your time. Please keep us informed of your whereabouts over the coming weeks, and do not leave the country, Mrs Mortimer. No trips to the south of France, if you please.'

I told him I'd be heading back to town, and gave him my aunt's address in Pimlico, and I saw a small moue of happiness cross his face. He was obviously as keen to get back to London as I was. The Detective Inspector headed out of the door, tipped his hat, flicked up his collar and walked away, up the lane, his figure blanked out by the snow as he disappeared into the whiteness.

Crumpet and I packed up. My case had been released to me because it hadn't been opened, or even taken into the bedroom, whereas Edward's had. The police had my details, they would be in touch. I looked out of the window and realised, with a thud of my heart, what a bad idea it would be, to try to drive to town in this snowfall, so Crumpet and I snuggled in front of the fire again. We would be spending another night, Christmas night, in the dreadful cottage, and I was glad that I'd packed a paperback. (An enchanting book about three women in the Italian Riviera, which took me out of myself for a while.) It was a long night.

The next morning was frosty, and I couldn't find anything to scrape my windscreen with, so I popped next door to ask. I knocked and heard nothing, although I was sure they were in. I knocked again, there was some distant whispering, and finally the door was opened a crack, by a middle-aged man.

'How can we help?' he asked, attempting a smile.

'Happy Christmas,' I said. 'Or... Happy Boxing Day... I um, I wondered if you could help me with my car, only the weather, you know.'

The man edged his way out of his home to have a look at the car, and the door was firmly shut behind him. When he returned ten seconds later, he had to knock on the door and explain to his wife that he needed something from his shed, before she would open the door and allow him back in – and back out. Within five minutes the motor was running and steam rose around us. I thanked him as he scampered away and, without looking back, he knocked on his door, was allowed back in, and that was that.

Crumpet stood on the passenger seat, paws on the dashboard, while I did my best to drive away from the first and last home that I'd had as a married woman, and as we swerved and slid past on unsteady tyres, the terrified neighbours looked on from behind their lace curtains.

The drive back to London was tiring – the car was surprisingly difficult to handle, and we stopped at a tea shop halfway. It was so crowded with holiday hikers, that it would require no small talk on my part. Crumpet devoured her ham sandwich, while I pecked at mine. It was cheese and mango chutney.

We got back to town, and my heart was warmed at the sight of the crowded city streets. Streets that knew nothing of the two days I'd just experienced. I did a fairly good job of parking, left my case in the car, and Crumpet jumped out of her seat and stood patiently next to me on the pavement when I rang the bell of the Pimlico townhouse, hoping that I'd got my aunt's whereabouts right.

Eleven

I knocked on the door, aware that all of my aunt's circle would have known not to have arrived unannounced at such an hour, and on Boxing Day too, and so, with no answer, I knocked a second and a third time and, just for a moment, I was reminded of the door that wouldn't open at the cottage, and the horrors behind it. Fortunately, Maude opened the front door before my mind was allowed to wander any further, and Crumpet and I were ushered inside as my aunt sashayed down the stairs, in her peach silk dressing gown and slippers.

'Georgiana! You're back! But, of course! I thought there was a chance that you might... well, anyway, it is lovely to see you, my dear, although your mother will be terribly disappointed that she missed – OFF! OFF!'

Despite my best efforts, Crumpet's little teeth snapped at her feather boa. 'Sorry, auntie,' I said, while Maude took charge – suddenly, I didn't quite have the energy.

'Terriers are so very lively, aren't they? OFF, CRUMPET!' said my aunt, and the change in her expression as she looked up and took a proper look at me, is something I shall remember all my days. I suppose I must have looked like someone whose one-day-old marriage had tragically collapsed. My going-away outfit had lost its crisp lines, my shoes looked like I'd played a game of rugby in them, my hair was a sight and oh! My stockings!

My aunt took her chatter down a notch and stuffed the feathers into her pocket. 'I'm sorry, my dear, as I said, I'm afraid you've missed your mother. She sailed back to Mexico yesterday, but we are absolutely delighted to have you back, aren't we, Lawrence? Lawrence!' she yelled. 'Oh. I'd forgotten he's gone west too – well, we all did, to be fair. We spent Christmas morning at the estate, and we've come back into town and – oh. Are you all right?'

I began to crumple a bit so she took me by the elbow and led me inside. 'I haven't l-left him,' I said, while Crummy scratched at my shins.

'Oh! Is Edward out in the motorcar?' Aunt Bathsheba mouthed the words, afraid that she had already said too much, and glanced over my shoulder. Taking the boa from her pocket, she wrapped it around the dog's collar, as a make-shift lead.

'No, Auntie Sheba,' I said. 'I'm afraid he isn't anywhere.'

'Maude? Ah, there you are. If you could take the dog away – give her a bone or whatever it is she eats and try to keep her away from the cats.'

'They are busy upstairs, having a go at my half-finished Fair Isle jumper,' said Maude, with a look that only a Persian cat could survive.

'Right. I am sorry to hear that, I shall have words with Gilgamesh and Xerxes later. And if the humans might have a pot of tea and a plate of shortbread in the drawing room, please?'

Holding my aunt's soft, warm hand, I was led up the stairs, and planted, shivering, in a chair next to the fireside, with a blanket over my knees. Satisfied that I was cosy, she turned her attention to the Christmas tree, all the better to primp its decorations and have a little natter while we waited for our tea.

'Well, we had a super Christmas,' she said. 'Aside from that bottle of liqueur your mother brought with her. My gift, would you believe? It was called "Tequila". Now, I am well able to hold any amount of sherry and I do enjoy a nightcap, but this was a step too far, and I wonder whether the headache is part of the gift. The Christmas morning birdsong was not welcome, as you can imagine, and the less said about the tractor sounds, the better. Ampney Tet was looking lovely, of course, although Maude tells me that eleven of the twenty-one bedrooms leak when it rains, and I'm sure you can imagine how cold it was. In fact, the ice house is warmer than our room, but well, we survived!'

I may have let out a little squeak at that point, and she turned to me briefly, before Maude entered the room with a tray of tea and biscuits. And as soon as she'd gone, my aunt said, 'Now, Georgiana dear, tell me, how was your honeymoon?'

'We arrived in Cherwell –'

'Did you say Cherwell? But, that's a stone's throw from Ampney! For a honeymoon? Oh, I am sorry, please do go on,' she said, still rearranging the decorations.

I took a deep breath, and told her, 'We arrived – in the Cotswolds – and Edward was murdered.'

The bauble dropped from her fingers and smashed, delicately, on the parquet flooring. The door opened again, and Maude entered with the sherry decanter, which she handed to me while she swept up the glass pieces with a handkerchief out of her top pocket. I took a swig and we waited for Maude to leave.

'Here, have a piece of shortbread, and if you could go over that again, that would be helpful,' said my aunt. 'I very much hope that I didn't quite catch what you said.'

We drank (out of glasses) and nibbled the little biscuits, as I told her the whole sorry tale. It had been a long couple of days.

Twelve

I finished my story, and my aunt sat silent for a moment, until Maude entered, to tell her that she had made the necessary excuses to Gillian Fotheringay. 'I've told her you're unwell, ma'am.'

My aunt flinched, and explained that Gillian is a bit mean on the sherry and gin front, and if anyone complains of any kind of illness at all, she always assumes it is down to "excess". 'It is annoying,' she said, 'And all the more so because Gilly is so often right.'

'Ah.' I rose from my chair, to stretch my legs, and my aunt asked Maude to bring us a fresh pot of tea, and she ordered poached eggs for our lunch.

When I sat down again, she patted my hand. 'Well, Georgie, I wasn't a huge fan of the man, as you know, but dying by blade... it's rather romantic, but in the very worst way. And you're absolutely sure he didn't fall on his sword – you know – decide he couldn't go on? Oh, I am sorry, I'm sure that Edward was absolutely elated to have caught you, it's just...' She passed me the plate of shortbread. I took one. 'Anyway, how are you feeling, my dear?' And when our eyes met, she swiftly backtracked. 'Shocked, of course you are. Don't worry, Georgie dear, you don't have to talk about it any more. Married a day – it's all so extraordinary.'

I nodded slowly. 'It is, auntie. Oh, and I've given the police your address.'

'You've –' The shortbread in her fingers sagged. 'Oh, yes, yes, of course. And you must stay here as long as you like.'

'Thank you, Auntie B, but I was thinking of going back to the apartment for a while.'

'Edward's apartment?' she asked.

'Oh. Do you think there'll be a problem with that?'

'Well, it was his, and you and Jack were only staying in it in the run up to the wedding.'

'Yes, perhaps you're right.'

'Where was he staying while you were there? You never did say.'

'I think he was bunking on a friend's floor for a few weeks, something like that. One of those chums of his from the wedding, I expect.' As I said it, I realised it sounded a bit ropey, and I hoped that the police, if they came looking for more information, would not ask me exactly where my fiancé had been living prior to their wedding day. I really should have known.

'You've no idea at all?' she asked.

'It just didn't come up. *He* always came over to visit *me*.'

'I would just like to put it on record, that I wasn't entirely comfortable with you living in the apartment belonging to your betrothed prior to your marriage, Georgiana, even with Jack as your chaperone, but you are your own woman. You always have been. And the only good thing about that whole business was that I gather Edward didn't take to Jack. He barely visited at all, did he?'

'It was all above board,' I said. 'He told me he preferred his women to drink sherry, although admittedly, probably not straight from the decanter.' I took another sip, sighed and shrugged. 'I was very happy to be married, have a wedding, be a "Mrs". And Edward Mortimer said we would have fine, long-limbed children, and I suppose he was right...' I said. 'But, really I'm not sure what to think or feel now.'

'Well, there's the New Year to get over, nothing happening between now and then. I should settle yourself down, stay in the warm, out of sight for a bit and try not to think about it.' As my aunt reached for the bell, Maude poked her head round the door, and told us that I had a telephone call, so I followed her out to the hallway.

Just two minutes later, I was back in the nice, comfortable, warm sitting room, with its lily-tiled chimneypiece, its beautiful Kashmir carpet and its deep, plush armchairs.

'There won't be any "not thinking" about it, I'm afraid. That was Inspector Routledge calling from Woodstock, and he informs me that the findings of the post mortem are in, and the coroner will hold an inquest next week.'

'Ah,' said my aunt, attempting to pour herself a Darjeeling, and completely missing the cup.

Thirteen

The inquest into my husband's death was to be held in Gloucester three days later.

I was required to attend, and I would undoubtedly be asked to give evidence. As far as the authorities were concerned, I was the last person to have seen my husband alive although, as I told my aunt, that could not be, and I explained that Edward must have been alive before he was dead, and in order for that to have been the case, whoever had made him dead must be the last person to have seen him alive. Somebody had murdered Edward, and if the police didn't have any luck finding that person, they would turn to the next best suspect. And, unfortunately, that was Mrs Georgiana Mortimer, née Wren. That was me.

The next three days were spent trying to keep calm, in my aunt's house in Pimlico. It wasn't easy. I spent most of my time hiding in the suite upstairs, while visitors came and went, wanting to know what had happened and how I was managing through the ordeal. According to my aunt, few of the guests seemed to have heard about what had happened, and only a couple of the visitors asked for their wedding presents to be returned. 'They can be a tight little bunch,' she said, 'But a suitable cock of the head, a steeliness of eye or a carefully-worded telegram soon sends them packing.' For the most part, the wedding guests who knew what had befallen the groom, expressed much sympathy for me, but none of them was in the police force, so that was no real help.

And Uncle Lawrence? I asked my aunt where he'd disappeared to, and was told that he was at his club, doing his best to ensure that this story stayed out of the papers.

'My understanding is that the Paternoster Club is for members of the publishing trade,' said Aunt Bathsheba. 'Paper merchants, print machine manufacturers, copywriters and so on, but they have been known to allow in the odd editor and newspaper man, because if anyone can afford the fifteen guinea a year fees, they can.'

'FIFTEEN?'

'Quite. Anyway, regardless of what one thinks of them – and the amount they're prepared to pay for such a place, they can be quite useful. And of course, the other thing occupying your uncle's time, is the funeral. If that could be done and dusted without the press finding out, it would be a miracle.'

I nodded, afraid that any word I uttered might turn into a sob.

The day before the inquest, Mr Stone arrived, with a large attaché case. He is a man of many parts, a legal expert, a second cousin of sorts, and one of my Uncle Lawrence's oldest friends. And according to Jack, he is also either a fan of Regency Romances – or of Lettice (who writes them).

Mr Stone sat at the dining table and opened his case to reveal a blank notepad on which he made strange "short-hand" squiggles while I told my story from beginning to end. When he put his pen down, the lawyer looked a little crestfallen.

'You believe that you were followed into the village, by someone on a motorcycle?' he said, 'But you don't know who was riding it, where they came from or what the make of it was?'

'It wasn't a Brough Superior, because that's what Jack rides, and it didn't sound the same.'

'So, you've no idea who killed your husband?'

I shook my head.

'And no idea why it was done?' He looked perplexed when I wanted him to look relieved. (Relieved that I hadn't done it.) 'And you say you also have no idea what the contents of Edward Mortimer's will are, or how much money he had.'

'Well, Georgiana's husband owns – or rather, he owned – a flat in Belsize Park,' said my aunt.

'Oh, very nice. Did he own it outright, or was it purchased with a loan?'

Ah. My aunt looked at me, and all I could do was shrug. We could see that the two things were very different.

'And none of this has anything to do with trusts?' he asked.

'I trusted him!' I said. 'Of course, I trusted him – I married him!' But even as I said it, I wasn't sure that I'd sounded entirely convincing, and besides, that wasn't what Mr Stone had meant.

'Trusts law,' he said. 'Not "trust". So, this matter has nothing whatsoever to do with planning your estate, inheritance duties or your will, Mrs Mortimer? Hm, that is a shame.'

While I looked aghast, my aunt patted my arm. 'Sadly not, Stone,' she said, 'If only it were something as straightforward as tax.' (And then it was the solicitor's turn to look aghast.) He put his files away, and thanked my aunt for her offer of a quick sherry, saying it was a little early in the day.

Aunt Bathsheba asked Mr Stone when we could expect to see him again. 'Well, I shall be in Gloucester tomorrow for the inquest, of course, and we shall see what the outcome of that is. You may be relieved to hear that my son is better equipped to handle this matter than I, should any further assistance be required,' he said, smiling proudly. 'He would be a boon to any hearing, however, he isn't available this week, hence my presence.' He closed his case, patted his pockets, located his spectacles and thanked Maude for the mint she offered him, from our Christmas bowl.

Sucking thoughtfully, Mr Stone went on, 'It would be nice if the inquest were adjourned, but I had a little chat with a col league who's more... familiar with these matters than I, and he tells me that country folk usually like to get things over and done with. However, I'm sure that if you tell the coroner everything you told me, Mrs Mortimer, omitting the bit about your hopes for a honeymoon in the south of France, it should be fine. Oh, and my condolences.'

He was offered another mint, and Maude followed him out.

'Well, I think that last little bit of advice was particularly pertinent,' said my aunt, with a cheery smile.

'Nothing to do with TRUSTS?' My voice rang out as we heard the front door close.

'Well estate planning is his speciality,' my aunt explained.

'If this were a matter of TRUSTS, I'd be delighted with him – I'd even TRUST him, but as it is, I'm not sure he's the right man for the job.'

'Well, hopefully there won't be any "job" for him to be the right man for,' replied my aunt. 'And he did say that his son would take over if there was any more of this silliness. Don't worry, my dear, they'll find out who did it. It will be absolutely fine.'

Auntie B poured us both a sherry and I hoped she was right.

FOURTEEN

Neither my aunt nor I had ever previously spent any time at Gloucester's court house, and we had no idea it was so peculiar – a classical Georgian building with two circular courtrooms. Edward's inquest was to be held in a much smaller room at the back of the building, and as we followed a court clerk through countless doors, Crumpet sniffed the hallways suspiciously.

'Is this used by the locals to regularly parade pigs and sheep?' whispered Maude, whose nose was also wrinkling.

We were shown into a small room with benches, and an impressively robust desk on a dais.

'Let us be grateful for this drab little room,' said my aunt. 'Much as I enjoy the time that we live in Pimlico, I am more than a little relieved that this inquest is being held far from the bright lights of London.'

I had to agree. We were a long way from the kind of people who are at a loose end in those odd few days before the beginning of the new year.

And if the few people we encountered as we entered the city of Gloucester were anything to go by, there were animals to be looked after and there was beer to be drunk. The local law court was not the place to be seen.

There were fewer than two dozen of us present, and that included me, my aunt, Maude and the dog, Crumpet. Uncle Lawrence was busy in the city (London, that is) and my aunt had asked Bettina, Lettice and Jack to stay in Pimlico. The ladies were keen to lend me their support, but Bettina in her black cashmere, Lettice in her lace and Jack in her leather and tweed might have been a bit much for this neck of the woods. My aunt had also suggested that the presence of a small dog might not be helpful, but Maude had insisted that Crumpet stay, saying that this was part of her training.

Moving along the bench, Aunt Bathsheba caught her stole on a nail and as I rose to untangle her, I noticed one other person in the room. It was Edward's nanny and, with a handkerchief held to her nose, she glared at me with red-rimmed eyes.

The inquest opened with the coroner's remarks about how unfortunate the timing of this incident had been, but his concern was for the people whose Christmas Edward's death had spoiled, rather than the fact that it had occurred just hours after our wedding.

The coroner established that the deceased was Edward Arthur St. John Mortimer, and then he called the constable who had accompanied me from the tavern, to state that the death had occurred at Cottage number two, on Whiteheart Lane in Mean Withering, on the border of the Mean and Greater Witherings, and to state the time that he had come across the body, and the amount of time it took to walk down the lane.

There was a loud creak as the door opened, and we all looked round to see the arrival of Mr Stone. How he has remained in my uncle's good graces with that level of punctuality, I cannot imagine. He was seven minutes late.

The constable then gave a report of Rodney's part in the discovery of Edward's body, and after clarifying the turn of events, it was Dr Charters' turn to give evidence.

'Isn't he the chap who was located at a party on a barge?' asked my aunt – rather too loudly.

I whispered "yes", and she told me – again, rather too loudly – that he reminded her of Douglas Fairbanks. 'The same rakish good looks and spring in his step, don't you think?' It was wholly inappropriate given the circumstances.

Dr Charters was asked to give a time of death, and he explained that it was difficult to establish due to the temperature of the cottage when he had arrived, but he stated that his findings did not contradict the statement that had been given by "the widow".

Gosh. That was the first time that word had been used, and I felt my heart slow for a moment. How awful it all was.

And when the gentleman had finished giving his evidence, he left the stand, and mouthed something to the coroner which may, or may not, have been "See you on the tee tomorrow", with a light swing of his arm.

The next witness to be called was the medical examiner, a rather stern-looking man called Shaw, who gave us all far too much detail about the various organs he'd examined. So much detail in fact, that the coroner asked him to "take it down a notch". We gathered from the dreadful doctor that there were no signs of poison, and that his findings were that death was not due to natural causes, but rather the sword that had been found in the victim's chest.

'I hope that man hasn't been paid for his time,' said Maude, and I couldn't help but agree.

The coroner stated that further enquiries had been made around the Mean, Little, Lesser and Greater Witherings. Nobody had seen us arrive, nor had they seen anyone else wandering about.

When Inspector Routledge was called up, he stated that the police had asked the landlady at the King's Head near Aylesbury, about our brief visit en route to our honeymoon destination. Reading from his notes, Routledge said, 'The landlady, a Mrs Evie Westwater, has said that after a late lunch of sausage rolls and hot cider, the couple had an altercation about their dog, and that they left the establishment on bad terms.'

An altercation?! And when the inspector said that one of the regulars at The Green Man had made a statement that I had threatened to murder my husband, I objected strongly, and was pulled back down to my seat by Maude.

And then it was my turn. I was asked about my relationship with the deceased, and I went over the story of our very brief engagement and our almost imperceptible marriage, our journey from town and our arrival at the cottage – possibly followed by someone I couldn't describe.

The coroner consulted his report. 'As noted earlier, the police asked the landlady at The King's Head about your brief visit, and she said that you and your husband had an altercation about the dog, and that you left the establishment on bad terms. Is this true?'

Unfortunately, I hesitated just long enough to confirm what he'd just said, before saying, 'I think "bad terms" is a bit strong'. I saw Mr Stone wince, and I heard my aunt ask him how things were going, and he smiled at her in a way that suggested he either had some work to do on his smiling, or that things were not going well at all.

The coroner went on, 'And according to the findings of Inspector Routledge, and the questions he asked of the regulars at The Green Man, you stated that you were feeling "murderous".'

I explained to the gentleman that it was to do with my having to chase the dog up and down the dark lane in the snow – and Crumpet didn't help matters by being curled up in a ball at Maude's feet, as if butter wouldn't melt in her mouth. This – the best-behaved dog in the world, had made me feel murderous? Impossible, surely? My explanation that I was cold and tired and annoyed (and not in the south of France) didn't get me anywhere, and when I added that I was a city girl and I complained that a few days in the Cotswolds – a part of the world that I was all too familiar with – wasn't what I'd been expecting in the way of a honeymoon, it didn't help matters. Strangely, it was only the inspector, who was sitting in the row in front of Mr Stone, who appeared to have any sympathy for my plight.

I was then asked to describe the scene when I arrived at the cottage. Holding on tight to the stand in front of me, I told them how, when I returned to the cottage with the milk, I heard banging upstairs, and had gone up, found the door closed and gone to get help.

'So, you say you heard sounds upstairs? Of an altercation?'

'Yes,' I said.

'Although the constable says that the window was open, and it swung shut in the wind. Could that have been the source of the noise?'

'I suppose so.'

'I'm sorry?'

'Yes, yes, it could.'

The coroner turned to the inspector, who confirmed that only two sets of fingerprints had been found on the murder weapon. Those of the deceased, and his new wife. I was asked to step down, and I returned to my seat, next to my aunt.

She asked Mr Stone his thoughts and he said, 'The where, when and how have been established, but not the who has done it – or the why?' He rubbed his luxuriant sideburns. 'Where a death is unlawful, there must be a killer, and where there's a killer, there must be more questions asked, and... a conclusion come to.'

As the inquest ended, I noticed Nanny scuttle out before I could disentangle myself from Crumpet's lead.

Baxter drove us back to the Pimlico townhouse in silence, which, with him at the wheel, was a four-and-a-half hour drive from Gloucester. It had been a long day, but when we arrived my aunt evidently decided something had to be done. 'We've still time to catch the Ritz if you'd like to blow the cobwebs out of your hair, Georgie?'

I told her I really wasn't in the mood, and I crept off to bed.

Why, oh why had I mentioned the south of France?

FIFTEEN

There was a firm knock at the door, it opened, and a squeaky little voice piped up, 'You're nicked!' Sitting on the stairs, I peered through the banisters to investigate, and I saw Maude standing on the doorstep, with her arms crossed, tapping her foot, while an inspector remonstrated with the little boy who had sneaked up behind him and his constable, after they'd knocked.

'Is there anything the matter, Maude?' asked my aunt.

'No ma'am, just the child who belongs to the people round the corner – having a little joke with the bobbies here.'

The boy standing behind the two policemen was one who enjoyed "hanging about". He was a child given to much casual snooping and if he'd lived in Mean Withering, I had no doubt that he would have seen me and Edward arrive AND seen who had followed us into the village too.

'Now, now, sonny,' said the constable, 'That is not the way we conduct ourselves, My apologies, ladies. It isn't correct and it isn't professional, and the commissioner would not be impressed. Been watching too many films perhaps? Too much time at the pictures?' He patted the little boy on the head. 'Go on, off you go.'

There was a sudden rumble of thunder and the granite-grey sky began to weep sheets of rain. My aunt invited the two gentlemen to take a step indoors, and I sat three steps higher up, all the better to hide.

'He's a naughty little creature!' said Maude. 'Not the words anyone wants to hear I have to say.'

'Indeed, madam,' said the older officer, looking awkward. 'Actually, it was Mrs Georgiana Mortimer we wanted a word with, if you would be so kind.'

I got up, and did my best to look like I'd been on my way down. 'I am she!' I said, speaking with a confidence I didn't feel.

'How do you do – yes...' He coughed into his handkerchief, and then stowed it away in his pocket, before fishing out his notebook. 'Mrs Georgiana Mortimer, I am here to arrest you for the murder of your husband, Edward Mortimer. I must inform you that you are not obliged to say anything unless you wish to do so, but whatever you say will be taken down in writing and may be given in evidence.'

'Corr!' said the boy. The little blighter hadn't gone away – and he had been right after all.

'Oh, I –' I held my aunt's elbow for a moment as I wobbled, and when I felt safe on my two feet, I popped off to change my shoes, while Maude offered to fetch my coat, scarf, hat and a handbag.

'You're not going to take her NOW surely?' said my aunt. And when she saw the embarrassed expression on the constable's face, she went on. 'But my niece has only just got up! Where are you going?'

'We're off to the Belgravia station, madam. Gerald Road.'

And with that, I was covered with a large police cape, and bundled out, protected from the rain. Aunt Bathsheba trotted out alongside the officers, as they invited me to sit up front, saying it was more comfortable than the back of their Black Maria. The whole thing would have looked a lot less dodgy if the officers had arrived in an ordinary street car, rather than this black police van, but I was grateful for their kindness.

The neighbours had undoubtedly seen everything, even so my aunt called out, 'Good luck with your investigations, dear!', but the matter wasn't helped by the way they held my elbows as I got into the van, and the way Crumpet clamped her little fangs around the constable's leg.

Doing my best to look as if I were an *arrester*, rather than an *arrestee*, I took my place on the front seat, while the snarling, howling little dog was scooped up by Maude, who informed my aunt that she would put the kettle on.

'We may require something a little stronger than that,' said Auntie B. 'I'm sure it's all just a formality, Georgie. There is obviously some mistake, and I'm certain you'll arrive at Belgravia Station, be greeted by Inspector Routledge – or someone of that ilk, who will offer you a nice cup of tea and an update of the current investigation and then give you a ride home. In the meantime, I shall give your Uncle Lawrence a call.'

I nodded, doing my best to smile. I didn't want my aunt to worry – and in an ideal world, she would have been right. The door slammed shut, and we drove off to the station.

Sixteen

Gerald Road Police Station is London at its best, worst and most interesting, and on this occasion the entire city seemed to be in attendance, and that included me.

A *lady* (I hesitate to use the word) wearing a dress with the kind of neckline I last saw on my Great-Aunt Christobel in 1908, was having a sing-song with a "Bright Young Thing" who was wearing a tartan silk dressing gown, and holding a cat that was smoking a pipe. There were three young men in three different team shirts, who were covered in mud and bloodied bandages – and three young constables doing their best to keep them apart. But by far the most frightening was a much older man, who was very neatly sitting in the corner – his face expressionless, as he watched those around him. Not a glimmer of surprise, fright, disgust or amusement crossed his face as he evaluated all the troubled souls that surrounded him. I couldn't help shivering as he looked me up and down.

I was grateful to be rushed through the throng, and allowed behind the desk. The sergeant on duty asked me my name, address and various other details, and while I was waiting for whatever happened next, I saw, or rather, I heard the arrival of my aunt.

She must have felt the same way I did, because before she'd even seen me, she approached the desk sergeant, and told him, sotto voce, that there was almost certainly a murderer sitting in the corner, next to the woman with the ferret up her sleeve. The officer thanked her for her assistance, and she assured him that she was a very good judge of character, and then she told him that she was my legal counsel, and let him know exactly who she was married to, and certain people with whom she played bridge.

'Aunti- Bath-MRS GODFREY! I'm over here!' I said, as I was led through the doors, and down a dark and dingy corridor.

The rain was lashing down outside. The sky was gunmetal grey, and small, mean little windows located too high to be useful, allowed very little light in. From behind (thankfully locked) doors, I heard words I don't often hear if I can help it, and sounds that were frankly disturbing. I was bundled into a cell, and ten minutes later, the little slot in the door was opened and shut, and I heard the words, 'As Legal Counsel for Mrs Georgiana Mortimer, I demand to be allowed in IMMEDIATELY!'

The door was unlocked by a weary-looking policeman, and my aunt was allowed in.

'Whoever you are, you've got five minutes,' said the officer, closing the door behind him.

'Well,' said my aunt, 'If this is one of the station's nicer cells, which was the kind of service Lawrence had been assured that you would receive, then I do not want to imagine the state of the others. And you'll be pleased to hear that I've already solved one crime this morning, but unfortunately, it wasn't yours. Now, what do you think of my disguise? Your uncle would NOT be pleased if he knew I was here, so I thought a little creativity was called for.' She held her arms out, all the better to reveal her costume. 'It's one of Jack's suits. Don't you think I look rather legal?'

'Is that your idea of in cognito!' I asked – I was genuinely intrigued. 'How did you get it on?'

'A minimal rolling up of the sleeves and trouser legs was required, and I assume that tone was related to your current circumstances, and nothing to do with my attire. I think I look rather dapper.' The seams were being tested, and she didn't take a seat, presumably afraid that something might tear, but I was very glad to see her.

'THREE minutes, ladies!' said the guard, and I had to agree. The longer my aunt spent in that suit, the more chance there was that the jacket and trousers might burst off and leave her in the altogether. Aside from anything else, my worry over the state of her dress, had pushed my very real concerns to the back of my mind.

'We're doing our best to find Mr Stone. He is almost certainly at Der Rosenkavalier or something, and you know how that drags. He does love a matinée. I've sent Jacqueline, in one of my dresses, to fetch him over here. You know how fierce the doormen on the Royal Opera House can be.'

'I'm not sure that Jack in a frock is going to help my cause, and given my current circumstances, I'm also beginning to think it might be time for a lawyer who specialises in something other than inheritance duties.'

'I do see what you mean, and I'm doing my utmost to address that little problem. I've also picked you up a little bar of chocolate, and your stole to keep you warm.'

'Thank you, Auntie B. You're very kind,' I said, and my voice may have wobbled at this point, because hers wobbled a bit too.

'I've left a tin of pâté and a packet of cream crackers with the desk sergeant, and he's promised he'll pass it on to you when it's been checked.'

I took a deep breath. 'I don't know why you've come, auntie, this is all just silliness.'

'TWO minutes, ladies!' bellowed the constable.

'I agree, absolutely, it will all blow over.' She gave me the lacy, embroidered handkerchief from her top pocket. It was entirely at odds with the suit she was wearing, and I had more need of it than she did. 'And your uncle is doing his utmost to ensure Fleet Street don't get wind of this unfortunate little matter, and he's been speaking with a couple of men at the Paternoster, who are newspaper editors – ghastly people they shouldn't have allowed in, but thank goodness, they did. You see it will all be worked out. Things could be a lot worse.'

Despite what my aunt had just said, I didn't see how they could be a lot worse than having one's husband be murdered on one's wedding night and then be hauled off to the police station as a suspect, and that must have shown on my face. She went on, 'There's another big story breaking. A viscountess has been discovered blackmailing people, and there's been an incident in Westminster – the House of Lords, in fact – so the men of the press do have other fish to fry. And that may be the reason why you were picked up in a van, rather than something a little more sedate. Oh, and the good news is that your uncle has had a word with the local MP, and you've been granted leave.'

'For what?'

'For the funeral, tomorrow. Your uncle managed to arrange a late booking, which should keep things fairly quiet.'

'Edward's funeral...' I felt my eyes fill with tears, and I dabbed at them with my pretty little hankie. 'What a way to start the year.'

'Yes, well, things can only get better,' she said. 'And if you don't get a visit from your actual legal counsel tonight, I shall be round first thing with him tomorrow.'

Even with the prospect of seeing her the following day, saying goodbye to my aunt was one of the most difficult things I have ever done, and as I lay on that hard, itchy cot that night, assailed by the sounds of ribaldry and riot outside, it gave me some comfort to know that my aunt could hear the New Year's Eve fireworks too.

Seventeen

I had hardly slept a wink and, judging by the sounds outside my cell, Gerald Road station was in the same state of chaos it had been the day before, but I felt strangely alert when there was a bang on the door at half past seven, and I was passed a bowl of cold, unsweetened porridge. But, by the time my aunt arrived an hour and a half later, I was exhausted and ready to drop. And I was not prepared for her to arrive with a young man who, despite his luxuriant eyelashes, looked as tired as I was.

'Good morning, Georgiana,' said my aunt, turning to her companion. 'Really, Mr Stone, your father would have been up and at 'em an hour ago, banging on the police station's door asking for admittance!'

Given what I'd seen of the young man's father, I doubted that, and could only assume that my aunt was trying to gee him up. In fact, Mr Stone the Elder would almost certainly have been enjoying one of the Paternoster Club's famous breakfasts with my uncle, to discuss the matter at hand, I'm sure, but still.

'This is Mr Benjamin Stone. He is the son of the Stone you've already met. The Elder Stone and Lawrence are conferring elsewhere.'

'How do you do,' I said, and I hoped my hot cheeks weren't apparent, although, when my aunt handed me a paper bag full of clothes, my temperature changed, rather, and I stupidly said, 'But they're all black.'

'Yes, my dear, they are.'

'Am I getting out on bail?'

'No, not exactly,' replied Mr Stone, opening his briefcase. He brought out a sheaf of papers and, even in my confusion, I noticed how square and neat his nails were.

'I'm not being released? But why?'

'I made enquiries this morning after your aunt's call, and, well, they think you might strike again.'

'What? They think I'll find another man to marry and kill him too?'

'Marry?' he asked, and suddenly his complexion was as pale as mine.

'It's her husband she's supposed to have murdered,' said Aunt Bathsheba, and I had to wonder whether the man had read any of the paperwork in that fancy case of his.

'We were only married for eight hours,' I explained, but I realised it wasn't as reassuring as I'd thought it would be.

'Yes, yes, of course,' he said, rifling through the papers. 'It says here... mm, it seems that they weren't impressed that you drove Mr Mortimer's car from the Cotswolds to London, before they could impound it for evidence.'

'But, how else was I supposed to get to my aunt's house?'

'I'm afraid that the car wasn't yours to take, as far as the police are concerned.'

'I'm being quite serious, Mr Stone. How was I to make it to London from the Cotswolds, with a small dog, a suitcase and a half-full hamper?'

'By train.'

'By...?'

'Like everyone else who doesn't have a Sunbeam Tourer to hand,' he said.

'But it was – it was my husband's car!' I pointed out.

'I'm very sorry, Mrs Mortimer, but until the will is read and the probate sorted out, it doesn't belong to anyone and the car remains in custody. It looks like the authorities consider you a flight risk.'

'Oh. I see.' I sank back down onto my rough, mean little bed, I reached for the tea on my tray, and took a sip and, with other things on my mind, it wasn't what I'd been expecting at all. My usual weak, unsweetened Ceylon, no milk and a dash of cold water to cool it down, followed by a jug of hot water to pep it up when required, had been replaced with a mug of something milked, sugared and tar-like. (Of course, at that point, none of us were to know how much longer I would be drinking my tea like that.)

'Lawrence has suggested that staying in prison until the court case, might be a blessing in disguise,' said my aunt. 'And you never know, some of our acquaintances might think you're still on your honeymoon.'

'With a husband who has a sword sticking out of his chest? Rather inconvenient, don't you think?' I couldn't help sounding as bitter as I did and, given my circumstances, I think that was understandable. Still, angry was better than sad.

'I think Lawrence is assuming that they don't all know exactly what's going on, Georgiana. Maude pointed out that your Great Uncle Bernard thinks we're still at war with the Boers, so your little contretemps won't have made any waves at all as far as he's concerned. Anyhow, I shall get the Girls on the case. It's all a hideous mistake and we shall get to the bottom of it as soon as we can, but in the meantime – Mr Stone?'

'Yes, I'm sorry to say, your aunt is right. You will be staying in jail until your case comes to court.'

Neither my aunt nor I had expected Mr S the Younger to put it quite as baldly as that, and she gave him one of her stares, until he nodded in an encouraging manner, and went on to say, 'And I'm sure your stay won't be very long at all, Mrs Mortimer. There is indeed, much to be done.'

My aunt smiled in an equally encouraging manner. 'I shall send Baxter around in an hour's time to pick you up for the chapel and '

But young Benjamin was shaking his head. 'I'm sorry, it's the constables who are to give you a lift to the funeral this afternoon.'

'I'm going to be accompanied?'

'I'm afraid so.'

'I think you'll find the outfit in the bag entirely suitable, my dear, and a spritz of the cologne that Maude popped in there too will do you a world of good. According to your uncle, we were really very lucky to have got the appointment we did.' My aunt patted my hand, as the officer opened the door to usher the two of them out.

Not feeling very lucky at all, I remained in the room, still handcuffed to my chair, when Young Mr Stone returned a minute later, and was joined by Inspector Routledge who I had last seen in the Cotswolds cottage on Christmas Day. It was an odd sensation seeing him again in such different surroundings and, judging by the slightly embarrassed look on his face, I suspect he felt the same. The inspector explained that he had been transferred back to London to run the Withering end of the case from a closer spot, by which I took to mean, that he had moved closer to me, the only suspect they had.

'Just a few questions,' he said. 'I'd like you to take a look at this, it was found at the scene of the crime.' He handed me a battered and bent photograph of a young woman. She was nineteen or twenty, by the looks of it, and it was a studio portrait, the kind that young men in the war were sent by sweethearts back home. I had no idea who she was.

'Are you quite sure about that?' he asked. When I shook my head, Routledge told me that he suspected she was a woman from Edward's past.

'My husband was fifteen years older than me, inspector. I expected him to have past liaisons,' I said.

'And if she isn't from the past?' he asked.

'Are you suggesting that... what are you suggesting?'

'I think he's suggesting that jealousy might be a motive for m-'

'Thank you, Mr Stone,' I said, and I turned back to the inspector. 'And you think that I found that on the kitchen table, or something, and would have stabbed my husband of six hours with a sword as a result? Why, she could be anyone! She could be the cleaner!'

Even as I said it, I thought back to the state of the cottage when we'd arrived; she definitely wasn't a cleaner, but she still could have been absolutely anyone. And to think that the police had the temerity to accuse me of murderous jealousy, when Edward's killer was enjoying New Year's Day at large!

The interview was brought to a close, and the detective inspector left the room.

'Well!' I said, pacing back and forth, one step at a time.

'Hm,' said the young advocat. 'If we're going to get you out, we're going to need to know more about your husband.'

'If we're going to get me out? If? It surely isn't as serious as all that, I'm innocent!' Although, I was aware, as I said it, that I was locked in a cell, in a police station, with handcuffs on. To the untrained eye, I certainly looked guilty.

'If there's anything more about your husband you can think of, anything at all that would indicate who might have wanted to kill him, it would be as well to let me or your aunt know, Mrs Mortimer,' said the young man, as he packed his case. And, looking a little embarrassed, he said he had to go, because my aunt had promised him a lift to South Kensington.

Alone again, my cuffs were removed, and I picked at the crackers and pâté that my aunt had given to the sergeant at the front desk. There were no chisels or hammers hidden inside. Facts might get me out of prison, but my aunt's food parcels would not.

EIGHTEEN

I sat in the police car just around the corner from the crematorium. I had begged the officers not to park right outside, and they had been kind enough to acquiesce. My uncle drove past and a minute later, he trotted round the corner to have a word with me before the funeral began.

'The crematorium directors unexpectedly had an afternoon free!' he said, and for a moment, I wondered whether someone had come back to life.

'Was the graveyard all booked up?' I asked. 'Cremation is all very new wave and fancy, but I'm not sure it would be my first choice.'

But according to my uncle, Edward's will had stated quite categorically that, on the event of his death, he be cremated. So, Woking it was.

He explained that the police had all the evidence they needed as far as my late husband's body was concerned, and said that he thought it was just as well to get the funeral over and done with. Uncle Lawrence remarked that the newspapers regard the first of January as a slow news day (following a very fast evening the night before) so we would be left to our own devices. He was right, of course.

With five minutes to go, my uncle said he would see me very shortly and he trotted back to my aunt.

The policeman drove us slowly around the corner, and I closed my eyes for a moment, aware of the lovely sound of the gravel and the click of the car door. Under any other circumstances, that would have signalled my arrival at Ampney Tet, home from home, but not this time.

I opened my eyes, and was relieved to see nobody hanging around outside the building, although my aunt had apparently heard our arrival, as she sprinted down the chapel steps, as my car door was opened by one of the constables.

'You look lovely,' she said. I was wearing the black velvet skirt, cashmere jumper and silk stockings that she'd handed me in the morning, and which I guessed belonged to Bettina. There was also a hat; a neat little felt cloche lined with silk taffeta and decorated with a satin band, and a mesh veil. It was from Liberty's, and it was very beautiful and very much Bettina's continental style.

Stepping out of the car, I was quickly handcuffed to one of the young officers in charge, and my aunt swiftly threw her fox fur stole over our wrists and linked arms with the other young officer. The four of us slowly walked down the aisle in two pairs and we must have been quite a sight. We made it to the front pew, Uncle Lawrence scooted along, the four of us sat down and, looking around at the plain white walls, I reflected on what a change it was from the beautiful church I'd been in just over a week before.

The number of people on our side of the aisle was much reduced, of course, and on Edward's side? The annoying sergeant who had been at the wedding was present, and, of course, Nanny was there too. She sat on the far end of the opposite pew, as far from us as she could, weeping and blowing her nose, furiously. I could have cried too, but not for Edward.

The chaplain arrived and consulted his notes – something my uncle had scribbled on the back of an envelope, although the clergyman had the good sense to conceal the address and stamp under his fingers.

The hymns drowned out the sound of Nanny's weeping, and the organist played beautifully, more than making up for the sermon which was even more general than I had been expecting. I couldn't blame Lawrence for that, as it struck me how little I had known about the man I'd been married to for so short a time.

As the service drew to a close, the constable and I stood up, and there was an audible hiss of "Shameful!" from Nanny. She'd obviously misread the situation entirely, and under any other circumstances, it would have been quite funny. Sergeant King rose from his seat to offer me his condolences, but my aunt's fox stole slipped, to reveal the handcuff it concealed, at which point the military man abruptly stumbled away and returned to his seat – and I erupted in a blast of nervous sniggers which, only the shocked expression on the chaplain's face managed to quell.

My aunt and I were the first to leave (flanked by our Metropolitan companions) and, as we left the chapel and got to the steps, the constable continued on.

'Charlie! I'm sorry, Constable Graves,' I said, 'I just wondered if I might have a minute to myself, and perhaps say a few words of thanks to the people who came?'

He blushed bright red, nodded, and as I began to rearrange the stole, he undid the handcuffs and went to stand by the car we had arrived in. His colleague joined him, and my aunt and I had a minute together.

'That went pretty well,' she said.

'Auntie B, we need to chat with Nanny. She knows more than she's letting on, and nice as Mr Stone is, I'm not sure he's going to get me out of this hole,' I replied.

'Mr Stone's son? Oh, I'm sure he knows all the rules and regulations, Georgie, and he's certainly got an eye for detail. Ben was the one who pointed out to Lawrence that Edward was so firm on cremation.'

'Mm, why do you think that was?'

Our side of the family trailed out, and Aunt Bathsheba told Lawrence he should wait for her at the car, and I could see he was about to offer me a lift, when he suddenly remembered my circumstances, and she shooed him away.

Nanny still hadn't come out, so my aunt and I walked up the chapel steps and looked inside. She was the only person left, and she was still dabbing at her copious tears, and studiously ignoring the attendant asking her to leave. 'There's another service beginning in twenty minutes time, madam, and we have to change the flowers!' The man glanced over at my aunt and I, and she gave him a nod, as if to say, 'I'll handle this,', although I wasn't sure that she could.

'Nanny,' said my aunt, gently tapping her shoulder, 'How lovely to see you.'

The woman turned, and her sad, moist eyes suddenly screwed up. 'If it wasn't for your niece, none of this would have happened! My little boy would still be here.'

'You must believe me when I say that she had nothing to do with Edward's death.'

'And no tears to shed for Eddy, either!'

She was right of course, but then, one's feelings for a husband of eight hours, whose murder one has been accused of, are complicated. I didn't know what to think, but I needed her to know one thing. I took a couple of steps in and firmly told her, 'I didn't kill him!'

Nanny tutted and turned, muttering under her breath something along the lines of, 'As good as...' before the main door squeaked open again, and I heard the constables asking us all to leave.

As I was led to the car, I looked beyond my aunt to the gardens that surrounded the chapel and I saw, skulking in the bushes, a woman I had seen before – and she had been wearing black then too. I threw myself into my uncle's arms, making as much noise as I could, and as he comforted me, I whispered over his shoulder, at my aunt, who was standing by his side. 'Auntie! Bathsheba! SHEBA!' I hissed, 'Look, lurking under that yew. Aunt! It's that woman – the one who was sitting at the back of the church. She must have known Edward!'

My aunt nodded and headed in the woman's direction, but it was too late. By the time she managed to make it around the pear tree and over the box hedge, the woman in black had disappeared and when my aunt turned back, I had been extracted from my uncle's arms, and shown into the car. I was on my way and, as we disappeared through the gates, I looked back, and saw Aunt Bathsheba pick up the beautiful hat that I'd left sitting on the gravel, at the bottom of the crematorium steps. A thing that fragile and lovely wouldn't survive prison. It wasn't designed for that environment and I hoped that my aunt realised that I had my wits about me. A silk-lined cloche would be no help to me inside.

And as we drove through the town's streets, and then headed north, I reflected on what Nanny had said about none of 'this' happening if it hadn't been for me. What had she meant by that? How was I involved? All I'd done was marry the man.

An hour and a half after my husband's funeral, I was delivered, hatless, to Holloway, at His Majesty's Pleasure. The prison walls are a stain on the city, sucking the light and joy out of its surroundings, and I am its newest inmate.

Nineteen

Today has been quite the day and it's hard to know where to start. My less than a day-old marriage ended with the funeral of my husband this afternoon, and now I'm sitting in a cell in Holloway. I AM IN PRISON. After registration, I was given a change of clothes, and my black outfit was replaced by rough overalls. I have no idea what's happened to that rather nice skirt and blouse, and those silk stockings are now just a memory.

I'm in a cell on my own, but from tomorrow I shall be sharing. I have been advised to enjoy the solitude while I can. The mattress is hard, the walls, ceiling and floor are grey and I'm not enjoying this alone time. I'm in trouble, a lot of trouble. I know someone else killed Edward, I just have to prove it, although that's easier said than done when you're locked up, but Aunt Bathsheba told me that the Ladies are ready to help, if I can only point them in the right direction. (And she also said that Lettice wept, Jack told me to sleep with one eye open and Bettina advised me to make friends with some of the women inside. What a thought!)

I'm writing in the margins of my copy of the *Count of Monte Cristo* because, although the book's pages are crumpled there are

1,472 of them on which to write around the edges and, while Maude was gathering my coat, I hid a couple of pencils in the spine. They came from my aunt's bridge set, and they're thin enough to slip into the book without bulking it up too much, and they are a life saver.

I'm still not sure whether you're allowed pencils and paper in prison, but I'm not taking any chances. They may have taken my freedom, but I fervently hope they do not take my stationery too.

They could take Monte from me very easily, of course, but the prison warder on duty during registration, told me that she's in charge of the library, and when the registrar asked what the book was, the warder said very loudly that it was The Book of Psalms. So, Monte Cristo and I have survived the first little test of life inside intact.

Day 1 Inside.

It is important that I have a record of my life here, in case anything should happen to me, and although I am determined not to dwell on its darker corners – it goes without saying that this is not a safe place. Despite the vaguely cheery tone of yesterday's diary entry, I barely slept a wink last night and I allowed dreadful thoughts to intrude, dragging me down to places I dare not consider. Unless one is at the Savoy enjoying cocktails at the American Bar, three o'clock is a wicked, wicked time of night to be awake, but three hours later I was feeling more positive, and that's an attitude I intend to maintain. I have no other choice. My solicitor is very nice to look at, but he may not be the right man for this job, and my well-meaning relatives also require guidance if I am to prove my innocence.

I shall write as much as I can, although the less written about breakfast, the better, except that it was not entirely cold. Thank goodness Jack and I lived – and cooked – together. My tastebuds have known deep disappointment and it is not a foreign experience. In fact, I find it strangely comforting, and it has occurred to me that Jack might have learned to cook inside. There are a lot of things I don't know about her – or the other ladies, when I think about it. (And lunch was also not *entirely* cold.)

Uncle Lawrence visited this morning, and he looked absolutely terrified – afraid to catch the eye of anyone present, but just as frightened of not knowing exactly where they all were in relation to him. My uncle has always felt safer in the presence of men, and it is one of the reasons he so seldom visits the Pimlico townhouse (despite its proximity to Westminster), so this is difficult for him. He is much safer in the countryside or the Paternoster Club.

In a bid to reassure myself as much as my uncle, I told him, 'They're not going to do anything dreadful to you. There are so many guards here, no one could lift a finger before they were stopped.' And he told me that it was the guards he was afraid of, and then we got down to business.

'Your aunt sent me to hear your plan. You always have a plan. Sheba said so.'

I took a deep breath and thanked my uncle for his vote of confidence, and told him to write down the next bit, and he was about to hand me his notebook, to make the notes for him, but the guard tapped our table with her truncheon. Uncle yelped, took it back and began writing. Poor man. I can't believe we're in the position we are. I told Uncle Lawrence about the woman I'd seen.

'She didn't come inside, but she was there at the beginning of the church service, and she was wearing black.'

'The chapel service, you mean?'

'No, she was in the church on Christmas Eve – at the wedding. She was there when you and I arrived, and she left rather abruptly when Rev Parsley asked "if there was anyone present...".' I told my uncle that I thought the woman had arrived for a funeral service, because of her black clothes, but that she had got the wrong day. And then I told him that I'd seen her at the crematorium in Woking too. I'm sure it was the same woman.

The warden yelled that we had 5 minutes left, and the level of chat in the hall went up a notch, everyone desperate to tell as much as they could while they had the chance. I told my uncle that she was tall – about my height and a few years older than me, perhaps. Her coat was a bit shabby, and I'm fairly sure her hat was knitted – not felt or fur. Whoever she is, she doesn't have any money for clothes. I had to check that he was writing all of this down (which is one of the reasons I'm writing it all down) because he'd begun looking nervous again.

To get his attention, I said 'Nanny thinks I'm guilty too – she said so!'

There was a snigger, and someone nearby said, 'We can't all be innocent, can we, darlin'?'

The warden called out that there was one minute to go before our time was up and, feeling suddenly desperate, I urged Uncle Lawrence to have a look around Edward's apartment.

He said "Righto!", and then made a face and added something about the property not being mine to investigate, but that he would ask Sheba – depending on how much bridge she had arranged for the rest of the week. I suggested it was time for him to go, and I got the feeling that he couldn't get out fast enough.

As Uncle Lawrence headed out of the exit, I burst into tears and heard a sudden yell, there was a sound of splintering wood and all hell seemed to have broken loose. I stumbled for the door and fumbling with the handle, I realised, too late, that it opened inwards and that there were three wardens on the other side trying to get in. I was slammed into the wall, and sliding to the floor, I felt someone pick me up by the lapels, there was a shout, and a fist caught my nose.

But that jolt did what a good cry couldn't, and seeing some woman charging towards me with the leg of a chair, I stepped to the side and gave her a violent slap – which was met with a look of surprise and a scowl, before we both fell to the floor in a heap, kicking, screaming and pinching.

By the time I was marched out of the visitors' room, I had blood streaming down my face from my nose – which one of the other inmates kindly reset for me. And I hope I shall never feel such pain again.

My nose, vaguely straightened, I was escorted out and told – in no uncertain terms – that I was being "let off" because I was new, and that this was a not-unexpected reaction to being incarcerated.

'It's also a very good start to your stay here,' said another of the wardens – one of the gentler ladies who worked at the prison. 'Tell them who's boss and it's less likely to happen again. You've probably made some friends!'

I wasn't entirely sure about that. As I took a last look down the corridor before stepping into my cell, I saw a small but solid-set woman staring at me with intent. Her arms rippled with muscles, and one of them was decorated with a tattoo of a bird's wing. With "friends" like that hanging about, I'm in trouble.

TWENTY

My first week in Holloway has gone by in a blur, and not just as a result of my two black eyes and my swollen nose. My new cell makes the room I spent my first night of arrest in, look like Claridges. And I'm sharing.

Ivy is the name of my cellmate. She is a large and frankly quite frightening-looking woman, but within five minutes of meeting her, I realised she is as gentle as a lamb, and has been badly mistreated and ill-used. Unfortunately, she insists on taking the top bunk, despite the metal frame's moans and creaks.

I asked her if she was absolutely sure it was a good idea for her to be the one up top and she told me, 'First time I've been up so 'igh. I've 'ad twelve cellmates and they've orways taken top bunk. An' so I fort maybe now it's my turn!'

I can see why she would feel like that, and was about to tackle the subject of our weight in a different way, when she poked her head over the side and fixed me with a steely gaze. 'You ain't worried 'bout me bein' too big for this, are ya?'

'No, no... it's absolutely fine.'

In our "free time" I lie on my bunk, trying not to think too hard about the bed above me and, because Ivy loves to listen to "a good yarn", I have taken to making up stories for her. I am also teaching her to read and write, and in return, Ivy has promised to protect me. I gather that most of the girls inside are fine. They might not return you the five shillings they borrowed – or if they do, it might not be legal tender – but that comes with the territory. When it comes to your personal safety though, for the most part, they are fine, but there are exceptions, according to Ivy.

'There's a gang of wimmin 'ere you might not wanna mess wiv, if ya know whorramean. They calls 'emselves the iggles.'

I should point out how difficult it is writing accents, but how important it is to really reflect what life inside is like. "There is a group of ladies here who aren't as affable as they might be. They like to be referred to as the Eagles," doesn't have quite the same ring to it.

Within a fortnight of arriving, I have less need of Ivy's protection, thanks to the hard work of another inmate. Whether I am sitting in a corner, reading a book, off to the laundry, or simply standing in line for a bowl of some mysterious stew, there is always a chance that Phyllida will show up, and "instruct" me in the noble art of self-defence. She was a suffragette twenty years ago and during her time in the organisation, she picked up a martial art called *suffrajitsu*. Phyllida's intention is to teach us all how to protect ourselves from insidious elements – whether they are the police, thugs, the Eagles, conniving shopkeepers or a dodgy man lurking around the corner. Phyllida is awaiting trial for shoplifting, and apparently, was found in possession of 25 pairs of tap shoes she hadn't paid for.

I am a keen pupil and Phyllida tells me I would have made front line material in any suffragette demonstration. 'But, since the Representation of the People Act, we don't have to march any more!' I said cheerfully. When Phyllida reminded me that prisoners do not have the right to vote, the smile was wiped from my face, and I wonder when the next election will be.

And if you're wondering why I've written so little recently, I shall tell you. I began making notes in *The Count of Monte Cristo*, and then realised I'd picked up the prison library edition by accident, and that's gone back into circulation. I am fairly sure I didn't include the date, my name or cell number in my musings, and according to my cellmate, there are at least 7 Ivys inside, so I should be fine. And to be quite honest, a lot of my writing wasn't the most hopeful and positive it's ever been. However, after being regularly jumped on by Phyllida, I am now much more aware of my surroundings and stronger, but I am also less able to sleep at night, although that could be a result of my upcoming trial. I have approximately seven weeks in which to find out who killed Edward, and it has been a while since Aunt Bathsheba came with any positive news, but she has told me to be patient.

When I'm not fighting my corner, or the fear of being found guilty, I am fighting boredom and stone walls. Already my recollection of wide, open skies, birdsong and a fresh, vigorous breeze, has faded away: replaced by shadows and the smell of cooked cabbage.

Phyllida's lessons are regular but generally broken up by the guards as soon as they notice them. It is difficult not to make a noise when someone is bending your arm behind your head, and teasing your elbow joint.

I have also joined the Cookery Club, which consists of a couple of ladies who used to run a café, describing the dishes they served – the ingredients and method they used to cook them, and their look, smell and flavour. It is a kind of torture, when one considers the gruel we are fed, and the fleeting feeling of bliss soon fades, leaving one feeling churlish. It's just as well that a session with Phyllida often follows.

Sunday

Last night, I couldn't sleep. The moon was full, and the light was keeping me awake – that and the fact that I now have approximately six-and-a-half weeks to prove my innocence.

I stood at the bars of my cell and, peering into the darkness, I thought I saw a shape. A figure was moving in the gloom, almost silent, and not in a way that a guard would. Whoever it was, was skulking in the shadows, listening, stopping and starting. I returned to bed even less able to sleep, my mind full of questions as to who it could be. An hour later, there was another sound, and I peered into the darkness, but there was nothing to see.

Tuesday

I am exhausted from having slept so little. I have neither seen nor heard anyone.

Wednesday

Aha! I have seen her again. It is definitely an inmate, and this time she was scampering along my side of the cells, and I got a smell of her as she walked past.

Before I entered prison, I hadn't thought much about the smells I 'wore'. I used rose soap in the bath, lily of the valley lotion during the winter when my skin was dry, and often used almond oil on my hands and nails, but jail is something different. Our baths are luke-warm at best, and if you are first, second or third in, you're lucky, added to which, we use carbolic soap, which my sense of smell stopped noticing after the first few days. The food we cook has been so thoroughly boiled, that it smells of almost nothing, and I dream of curried mutton and blackberry crumble with custard.

But this woman smells of something. I closed my eyes and took a deep sniff when she returned back the way she came, and realised that she smells of jasmine.

What do I know about her, apart from her scent? Well, she is obviously in a cell that lies in the direction of the laundry house, the opposite direction from the warden's office. She is neither particularly short nor very tall, and she knows how to get out of her cell at night. She can pick a lock. She is useful, and someone I really must get to know.

Thursday

Trying to find this mysterious prowler keeps my mind off the problem at hand. I have sidled up to everyone I dare to – whether to look over their shoulder at a jigsaw puzzle they are doing, a drawing they're etching into the wall, or a piece of sewing they're working at (under the exacting eye of Officer Styles, who, we're sure, sells the better examples). Finally, I sniffed a hint of jasmine – the merest suggestion of the flower. A memory that was imprinted into the rough cotton of the young woman's tunic. She is quiet, cautious and, I notice, she doesn't hang around with any one group too long. Where she does hang about is the library, and that is my next stop on the prison rota.

Twenty-One

'Have you any idea how inconvenient it is, coming all the way up here, Georgiana?'

It was visitors' day, and my aunt had been the last to arrive.

'It can be as much as an hour to Holloway from Pimlico depending on the traffic – and then there's the weather of course. Such thick fog, we almost had to abandon our trip!'

She did look flustered, and the fog had left her hair decidedly frizzy, although I could only dream of looking into the mirror, let alone seeing a reflection I didn't like. (Although I won't pretend there wasn't a certain freedom to that.)

'I am sorry, aunt, I shall do my best, next time, to be committed within a railway stop's travel of Belgravia.'

'I can't see why they couldn't have put you in Pentonville, Georgie, it is just a little closer.'

'Closer – and a man's prison,' I told her.

'Right. Just as well they didn't then, but it's so chilly in here. Fancy a snifter? Here we are – and It's not just any sherry, this is the best Madeira. Agostinho brought it when he came round to show your uncle his new racing car.' Aunt Bathsheba leaned over to offer me the flask, but the guard banged on the desk.

No consorting with the prisoners – and certainly no pre-lunch drinks.

'Your uncle has told me about his visits, of course, but how are you holding up?' she asked. 'And – has something happened to your nose? It seems a little... different. Anyway, I see that that shingled style of yours is beginning to grow out, which is a good thing in my opinion, but Lawrence said that you seemed a little down in the dumps, when he visited.'

'Down in the dumps?'

The warden raised her eyebrows, and I did my best to calm down. 'Down in the dumps? Yes, yes, I AM feeling down in the dumps. I'm in jail for a crime I did NOT commit, which is the most unsatisfying feeling in the world. My court case is coming up and... unless they find the actual killer, it looks like it will be ME who SWINGS for it!'

She flinched, the guard flinched and even I couldn't help flinching, and it took a moment for the chat in the room to resume. The guard looked the other way when my aunt patted my hand. 'Yes, about that. The Girls and I have been doing a bit of casual sleuthing to ensure that my favourite niece –'

'Your only niece.'

'– is released as soon as possible,' she said. 'We know you didn't do it, but we need your help, and according to your uncle, you've come up with nothing so far, apart from that woman and the flat. But you must have some ideas, Georgie – keen young brain like yours. Now, what did the police miss?'

I felt uncharacteristically vacant, and it must have showed, because my aunt banged the table with her lavender-gloved fist; something she immediately regretted.

'Jack has suggested trying to B-R-E-A-K you out, but I'm not sure it's an option, and as you say, time is of the essence. I can see that you're feeling a bit up and down, but you have to apply yourself. What did you notice? What was strange, unusual? We have to crack this before it comes to court, because your uncle's contacts won't be able to stop this from showing up in the papers then, and once those pressmen have a sniff of this story, they won't let you go.'

'Give me a moment,' I said, laying my head on the table. (I just wanted all of this to go away.)

She lightly thumped the table again. 'Edward was a mysterious man, and it wasn't just his age that concerned me. We knew very little of his movements and his background; he had no family to speak of, and a history of military service isn't enough to go on. Who his age hasn't served?'

I looked up at her. 'Well... there was one thing. I don't know where he spent his time when I was in his apartment with Jack.' My aunt handed me her handkerchief and, after I'd blown my nose, she suggested I keep the exquisite one-of-a-kind Belgian lace. (Her expression suggested that it would never be the same again.) 'One evening, he mentioned something about staying with a friend of his in Primrose Hill, but Jack always watched him leave – you know what she's like, and she said he took the road to Ealing.'

'How did she know?'

'He must have popped round the corner to pick up some tobacco, or a paper or something, because by the time she'd put her helmet and goggles on and got onto her motorbike, he was only just getting into his car. And she said that for someone on his way east, he was going in entirely the wrong direction. Her tap-dancing lessons are in Ealing, and that was where she lost him.'

'Right, well, it's strange and it's a start. I shall ask her about it. And we have that odd woman at the church and chapel to find, although I'm not sure how we're going to manage that. Anything else that might be of use?'

'TWO MINUTES LEFT, LADIES!'

'After I've done my time in the kitchen, I'm hoping to be put on the library rota. It's quieter there and there will be more time to think.'

'You will have to apply yourself, Georgiana, this whole thing is rather tricky, although we are fortunate enough to have one advantage the police do not.'

'What's that?'

'We know they have the wrong woman in their sights. We know you didn't murder Edward.'

'Thank you, Auntie B.' It was the best thing I'd heard in what felt like a very long time.

'And I shall thank you, when you've put that grey matter of yours to work. Oh, and you'll be happy to hear that we shall be visiting your pad in Belsize Park at some stage this week.'

'Is that allowed?' I asked, but she waved my concerns away.

'Jack has been chatting up one of the staff there, and she informs me that it's only a matter of days before we'll be able to get in without the police being notified.'

Edward had been keeping secrets in the weeks before he was killed, and I only hoped that Jack and my aunt would be able to dig something up. I wasn't sure what the significance of Ealing was as far as my late husband was concerned, but it was west of Belsize Park and, one might argue, en route to the Cotswolds.

'ONE MINUTE TO GO!' yelled the guard, and I urged my aunt to leave.

'It just so happens I am hosting a bridge game today, so it would be just as well,' she said, patting my hand. 'There is light at the end of the tunnel, Georgiana, so keep your eyes open, and know that you're not the only one looking. We haven't been entirely idle, we are on the case. That's the expression, isn't it?'

Twenty-Two

Monday

Working in the prison kitchen was a lot more stressful than I'd imagined, all the more so when I noticed the kind of women who'd been put in charge of cutting up the meat, wielding enormous great knives that they insisted be sharpened every single day, to "make them as useful as possible" (Dirty Dorothy's words, not mine). So, I got out of there as quickly as I could, but I don't excel at laundry either, and my hands are red-raw. If only I had a pot of hand cream. Some of the other inmates enjoy the heat and the ribald songs, but it isn't my scene, so I'm on a half-shift there.

It is a relief to have been moved to the library, which is cold and smells funny, but it is where I feel safest. I spend the day looking up lists of books, making recommendations and ferrying them around on a little trolley. It isn't the British Library, but it isn't half bad. (Thank goodness for Elizabeth Fry.)

There is nothing on the shelves that has been published by my aunt's company, nor my uncle's (relevant as current government legislation might be to the women inside). There is also nothing of a practical nature; no guides to building a makeshift ladder, leadership skills or "101 Knots". There are, however, a lot of religious tomes available, and an impressive selection of "light" romance. Nothing much to stir the blood but, above the slight mildew scent in the air, I noticed a hint of jasmine emanating from a dark corner that was dedicated to cookery. I sidled over with a pile of books that needed re-shelving, and gave the woman a quick smile – and took another sniff.

She was maybe ten years older than I, small with dark, curly hair, and a sallow complexion. I wondered whether she'd been in so long that her skin had forgotten the sun. I noticed she was gazing at the cover of the book I had in my hand, "Mrs Dodbury's Treasury of Sweet Treats, Puddings and Cake".

'Morning!' I said.

The spell broken, she glanced up at me, as if afraid that I would engage her in conversation. I had obviously approached this in completely the wrong way, so I shelved the book I judged to sit closest to her location, and hurried away, silently, to the sparse Foreign Travel section. (I wasn't sure that Merseyside, East Anglia or Jersey counted as "foreign", but clearly someone did.) I shall have to formulate a plan.

Tuesday

No library today, so I spent the day teaching Ivy her letters and trying to think. What, as my aunt had asked, had struck me as odd?

I considered the relationship I'd had with Edward, and for the first time, was thankful it had been as brief as it was. I'd had no time to forget any particulars, certainly. I thought back to our wedding day, and his guests. Those chums of his would be easy enough to find. City types – or army mates – who had a passing relationship with him that mostly consisted of an evening of drink at the club, and hiking at the weekend.

Edward's parents were long gone and, as he'd mentioned so many times, we would have lots of children, to make up for his lack of siblings. An only child and cousin-less, his side of the aisle had been fairly empty.

Then there was Nanny. His number one fan, his rock and stay. Always there for him. What was there about their relationship that was strange? Well, he still depended on her despite the fact he was a man in his mid-forties. She usually always called him "my boy", but now and again she called him "Eddy" (never "Edward"). When we'd first met, he'd told me that his father had also been called Edward so, to distinguish them, his mother had referred to him by the diminutive, and Nanny had done the same.

Was there anyone else at all?

Nobody, unless we included the woman in black at the back of the church.

Thursday

After a couple of days of circling each other, today I had my chance.

Mr Benjamin Stone came to visit yesterday to tell me his news, none of it helpful. Inspector Routledge has found no killer (other than me, of course), there remains no witness to the mysterious motorcycle and, more to the point, nobody who heard the sound of its engine.

Towards the end of his visit, Ben sneezed as if he were allergic to something. (Grey linen perhaps?) He fished his handkerchief out of his pocket, and managed to dislodge a packet of humbugs. By some miracle, they fell to the floor, at the exact same time that one of the inmates threw her chair over, and began a small riot. While the attention of the guards was turned to the other side of the room, I bent down, swept up the sweeties and shoved them down my tunic. I suspected they might come in handy when I was on the look-out for the jasmine lady.

I have worked out that when she isn't using the governor's eau de cologne, she must be moving in the direction of the kitchens, because I've seen her pass by, popping something in her mouth. There is little of interest in the kitchens, but I recalled the book on puddings that I'd caught her reading. Compared to a handful of raisins, my pocketful of humbugs is treasure. Much as I would love to scoff the whole lot, I immediately see their value – and today is the day. I have library duty after lunch, when I shall hopefully have more to write.

When I saw her at the library, she had finished her chores and with no readers to assist, she was crouched in the corner, flicking through a cookery book's sticky pages.

'I notice your interest in the culinary arts,' I said, 'And I wonder whether you know about the cookery club?'

She was about to bolt, when I thrust a humbug her way, on an open palm, and she grabbed it without a second thought. She'd unwrapped it and it was on its way to her open mouth, when she came back to her senses and realised what she had done.

'I'm –'

'It's yours. And I've more of them too, if you'll tell me how you're getting about the hallway at night.'

She looked terrified, until I offered her a second humbug, and that look of bliss returned. By the time she'd eaten three of them, I also had her "eating out of my hand", as it were. I have managed to convince her I am no threat, and I have introduced myself. I also volunteered what I was in for, which sealed the deal. It is the height of bad manners to ask after someone's crime – besides the fact that so many of us are innocent of course – so by admitting what I was awaiting trial for, I have revealed something I didn't need to. I also admitted that curiosity had got the better of me, and I was keen to know how she was getting around. While she gave it some thought, I offered her another humbug. I have seven left.

'You have to show me how you're doing it!' I hissed – and I realised I'd spoken far too loudly, so I carried on, even more loudly. 'Because I simply HAVE to know where you found that RECIPE FOR CHELSEA BUNS!'

She looked dumbfounded, and when the hubbub of "What IS she talking about?"' and "SHUT UP!" had died down, I tried again. 'Please show me how to do it! I'm cell 324.'

Before she could say no, I pressed a humbug into her hand, smiled and walked away.

I got my answer eight hours later, when she tapped me on the shoulder and woke me in the middle of the night. Fortunately, she had her other hand over my mouth and trapped my scream, otherwise we would have been joined by my cellmate, and that would never have worked out. Ivy's middle name is neither "Quiet" nor "Stealthy". (It is Perpetua.)

I followed my new friend, Marjorie, out of the cell, along and down to the door of the prison offices. She was, of course, incredibly light on her feet and very swift, and she had to return to me several times while I tiptoed my way along, trying in vain to make as little sound as she did.

When we arrived at the last door, we stopped, listened, she tinkered with the keyhole for about ten seconds – listening carefully, until we heard a 'click'. In the silence of the prison at night, it echoed through the hallway, and I scrunched my eyes shut – hoping that that would somehow deter anyone from hearing the sound – or seeing me. I felt a tap on my arm, the door was open, and Marjorie invited me through. We were in the office of the governor's secretary, and with another resounding 'click' we were through to the governor's office.

Twenty-Three

'How did you do that, Marjorie?'

'Easy,' she said, taking a seat at Governor Fraser's desk and twirling in the darkness. 'Fancy a cuppa?'

In the corner of the office there was a small gas jet and a kettle and she told me to fill it and put it on, and then gave me very strict instructions to listen for it boiling. If the kettle whistled it would be very bad indeed, and it was my job to keep watch, while she used her lock-picks on the filing cabinet. That was where the hand cream and the biscuits were kept. 'We mustn't eat too many, otherwise Fraser'll realise and be onto us!' whispered Marjorie, taking a handful of custard creams. After all, it was her sweet tooth that had persuaded her to listen to me in the first place.

The kettle neared boiling point, I whisked it off the gas and my companion made a small pot of tea and, while we waited for it to steep, I enjoyed the moonlight filtering through the window and the textures of the world beyond these walls. The Outside was a place I hadn't seen for weeks, let alone enjoyed. (And to think that there were women in Holloway who hadn't seen it for decades.)

As I took in the details of the street below, I realised how little greenery I had seen since I'd been arrested. I was used to living in the city, and London is a surprisingly green place to live, with generous parks and lots of tree-lined streets, but I had grown up in the Cotswolds; the same place I'd spent my ill-fated honeymoon. The area's rolling hills and soft greenery are like balm to my soul – until I've had enough of it and feel the need for double-decker buses and department stores – but living in a grey brick prison was something else. I looked over at my companion's pale skin and wondered how long it would take mine to lose its glow, and then wondered if it had already gone.

My partner in crime poured the tea, and while she waited for hers to cool, she looked over the items on the governor's desk, which was very tidy. A blank pad, a blotting sheet, a cup of pencils and a typewriter in the corner, which must have been stored in here for the secretary to use. There wasn't any sign of one in the outer office.

Marjorie took a pencil from the cup and, holding it sideways, she gently shaded over the blank piece of paper on the top of the pad. Holding the note up to the light, she said, 'Fraser's been to the theatre tonight, by the looks of it.'

'What?'

'It says so here. Two tickets for "Clowns in Clover".'

She showed me the faint outline of words; writing pressed into the paper from the sheet above, which had been discarded.

'Check the bins!' she whispered.

I knew better than to ask what for, and in it I found a piece of carbon paper. 'We'll have that,' she said.

'But why?'

'Information. It takes a moonlit night, but it'll be worth reading at some stage if there isn't anything else to look at, or a night when there aren't any biscuits.'

'The way you unlocked those doors – would you mind teaching me how you did that?' I asked.

'Why?'

'Just idle curiosity.'

'If you tell anyone else, I'll-'

'You can threaten whatever you like, I won't tell anyone. I promise.'

'It'll cost you!' she said.

'Humbug?' I asked.

N.B. This is my best recollection of the event, as my diary entry read simply, "Had a cup of tea in the office of the G with M." It was a long night, and I was rather tired.

We met the next three nights, and Marjorie evidently enjoyed showing off her skills, as much as she relished the sweeties I gave her in return. By the third night, the biscuits had run out, so we turned our attention to the carbon paper and, in amongst the backward "To Whom it may concern"s, and the "Yours sincerely"s, there was the odd gem of information. And that was how we learned that a new inmate was arriving soon, transferred from Broadmoor. She was deemed to have been cured, and would serve out her time with us in Holloway.

The thought of being "well enough" to go to prison, after ten years in an asylum, wasn't a happy one, and the letter said that Edna Anderson was joining us the following day.

'You might want to keep Ivy close for a few days until we know the lay of the land,' said Marjorie. 'Sometimes the women they transfer aren't as well as they'd like to think.'

'Maybe it's less expensive to keep someone in prison than keep them in an asylum?' I said. 'Anyhow, thanks for the tip.'

And with that, I gave her my last but one humbug, we tidied up behind us, and left the office.

That night I lay in bed thinking about ten years in an asylum, followed by prison. What a life. And I thought about Marjorie's complexion, the lack of sunlight, weather, greenery, the sound of children, the feel of cotton, silk and angora, the taste of a gin and tonic. All those things she'd spent so long away from.

And then I remembered that, if my court case did not go as I hoped, a lifetime in prison would be the last thing I'd get. My life would be cut radically short and I would have no time at all, anywhere.

And I think this next extract from my diary may go some way to illustrating my feelings at the time:

Hello Monte Cristo,

I haven't written for ages, and I wonder if it's because I'm getting used to life inside. Is that a good thing? I'm not sure it is. The food is always the same, the routine never changes. I have regular visits to the library, and I've got used to my bed, and I have friends, but one thing they don't tell you about prison, is the sensation of always being watched. My skin just itches at the thought of this constant surveillance, and I long for the countryside, not for the sake of the grass, birds and trees, but for the solitude that has been denied me so long.

There are wardens watching us, of course, but I feel like I am also under scrutiny by the other inmates. Solitary confinement is the only time any of us have to ourselves, and yet nobody is a fan of that part of the prison. The feeling of bustle is constant, and I imagine that for a lot of the long-term ladies here, not being surrounded (when they're released), must feel just as awful.

We are watched in the library, in the laundry, in the kitchens, in the canteens, when we troop around the yard, and when we have our baths. And in our cells, we are never alone either. I am lucky, at least, that Ivy is a sweet, sweet soul who loves stories and learning to read – and that my first impressions were not correct. Her frequent black eyes are down to her training with Phyllida, although, I realise as I write this, that I also had a couple of black eyes when we first met.

But there is one inmate who gives me the willies. She's shorter than me by a head, and she's fairly round, but she carries herself in a way that suggests she knows how to defend herself – and more. She's one of the ones with a wing tattoo on her arm, which must mean she's a member of the Eagle gang. There are plenty of women like that around, but they aren't generally watching me. This woman is. She's always watching, watching, watching. I hope very much I'm being silly about that, but thought I'd make a note of it in my diary, just in case.

Twenty-Four

Lunch was stew and mash, and although the clamour of voices was deafening, it seemed to be progressing in quite a civilised manner. (The day before, there had been a bit of a kerfuffle over some kidneys.) Doing my best to avoid anyone's gaze, I sat as far away from everyone else as I could, and set myself to thinking about the investigation. Aunt Bathsheba had told me her plans for the week, and I wondered whether her search of Edward's home had already finished, or only just begun.

The property in which I'd spent the run-up to the wedding, was a recently-built block of flats, located in a very desirable area, and its fashionably large windows afforded a beautiful view of its leafy surroundings. As the clatter of plates echoed around the prison dining room, I recalled the apartment's lush, cream-coloured carpeting, and its heavy curtains. And a sudden shiver reminded me of the bathroom's impressive radiator, the thought of which, failed to warm me up.

All in all, it was the latest thing in city-living, the perfect home for a couple of newly-weds. I tried to imagine Aunt Bathsheba rifling through the drawers and cupboards, although – thinking about it – I was sure that Jack, and maybe even Maude, would have gone along too, in which case my aunt would be the one asking questions and directing the action, Jack would be the one smoking out of the window, and Maude would be the one most likely to be doing the rifling – and enjoying every minute of it.

I didn't know what I wanted them to find, exactly, but I tried to "walk" my way through the apartment, in a bid to consider where they might look, and I began by imagining the hallway. Nothing very much to see there. A small cabinet that housed Edward's shoes and his extensive collection of fishing flies. The bathroom was smart but there was nothing out of the ordinary in its mirrored cabinet – and likewise the kitchen. It was a dinky little room, which was fitted with neat, white cabinetry that I had planned to paint green, as soon as we returned from our honeymoon. I didn't recall anything mysterious about it, and certainly, if there had been anything out of place there, Jack would have found it. She was a poor cook, unschooled, but very keen, and she would have opened every drawer and cupboard, and tried every utensil, I was sure.

The reception room was sunny and light (on days when it was sunny and light), but it was also everything one might expect of an unmarried man. It was a bit bare, perhaps, save for the odd pile of books (military history), and a steamer trunk with a flat top, that had been covered with an old woollen blanket (ex-army), and was used to store piles of newspapers. Edward liked to say that the room needed a "woman's touch", and for a moment my attention turned back to the decor of the dining hall, and the messages scratched into the tables.

Jack had been my chaperone prior to the wedding, and she had been put in Edward's bedroom. For some reason he had been quite firm about that, and I recalled a cabinet in the room that was locked. I had asked my husband-to-be about it, and he'd said he would find the key after we were married. Meanwhile, I slept in the guest room – the smaller of the two rooms, that Edward referred to as "the nursery".

It was a small, neat, modern little flat with no curious nooks and crannies, certainly no loft and little in the way of mystery about it or creaking floorboards. With the exception of that trunk, and the cabinet, the little home was far too new to have any skeletons in its cupboards. I shivered, and was brought back to the real world, when a chunk of potato landed in my hair. Taking my plate with me, I crawled under the table, and let the food throwers get on with it.

I only hoped that my aunt, Maude and Jack had thought to look in both of those places – and that they had managed to sneak in in the first place.

The sound of a metal spoon banging on a pan brought me back to the cold, dark brick of my current surroundings, and I stirred the lumpy gravy into my mashed potato and ate a forkful. It was, admittedly, better than anything I could cook, and for a moment, I wondered how many more stints I'd have to do in the kitchen before my court case came up.

The following day, when the warden gave out our post, I received an envelope from Cricklethwaite, Dingle & Stone (my uncle's solicitors) that contained a letter from my aunt – both of which had, of course, been opened. I was surprised they'd been allowed through, but suspected that my uncle's contacts might have had something to do with it, because there was nothing very subtle about my aunt's correspondence.

Dearest Niece,

I hadn't appreciated what an interesting little apartment that is – and Belsize Park so handy for town. If I'd known, I would have swapped places with you, and had you sleep in the townhouse. And the convenience of a modern kitchen! Jack and I toiled long enough to earn ourselves a plate of eggs and bacon, and watching Maude prepare our lunch was a joy. And then, of course, after we'd managed to eat it, I had to get the smell of bacon out of my hair, as I was due at a bridge game with my usual crowd in the afternoon. And if Cecily and I had been playing for money I'd be in Monte Carlo by now! We wiped the floor with the other pair and left the club cock-a-hoop, although Mary said she didn't think they'd agree to play with us again. Said something about our attitude being "off".

Anyway, back to the apartment. I had to get the smell of bacon out of my hair, so Maude ran me a bath, and oh! So warm! How wonderful those radiators are – and so much hot water. It's made me think twice about my place in Pimlico, I can tell you. I shall be informing your uncle that funds are required to modernise it, and I'm sure he'll be able to claim it as something or other at the end of the financial year.

Now, as far as our investigations go, Maude, Jack and I popped round to you-know-who's flat and – oh – I've already written to you about that, haven't I? Well, it WAS very nice, and we paid particular attention to the room Jack's staying in. She said she'd already had a go at the cabinet and the trunk and hadn't had any luck with either of them, so I had a go at them and I got nowhere with them either. Finally, we decided stricter measures were required, and Jack tripped over a handkerchief and landed on the trunk and then the chest. Unfortunately, the chest broke and we tidied up some very interesting paperwork and some other bits and bobs that we're looking into now, and which I'm quite sure will not be of use. And Jack was good enough not to take the remnants of the chest out too.

Keep your spirits up, it won't be long. We only have to find out who did the you-know-what, and you'll be O.U.T. in no time.

Much love, B

I wasn't sure what to make of that last couple of lines. There was a clock ticking loudly, tick-tick-tick, hammering my heart and teasing my neck. While a part of me imagined that it was the sheer injustice of being arrested and tried for a murder that I did not commit that would take me to my grave, there was a rather more obvious thing that would haul me off to eternity, and that was a conviction. The sooner we found another possible culprit – and found out what really happened to Edward, the sooner I could be dragged away from being dragged under.

And as to the "who" had done it, I wondered whether the "why" might lead us more swiftly to an answer. Why had Edward been murdered? I hoped that the papers my aunt had found would help in some way, and I tucked the letter under my mattress. I also wondered whether I'd read it right – was Jack staying in the flat?

And if anyone reading my correspondence was under the impression that anything underlined was a falsehood, they were almost certainly wrong.

Twenty-Five

One thing about prison was that when I wasn't working in the library, laundry or kitchen, and was safely tucked up in my cell and had read Ivy her night-time story, I had time to think. Too much time.

The more I thought about the last few months, the more questions I had. And I couldn't help feeling that my aunt had a point. The Cotswolds for a honeymoon. But why? It seemed like an odd place to go, given that he knew I'd grown up there. It's lovely to look at, but nothing new, and the cottage he'd chosen had been such a mess. I wondered how much or how little money Edward had – and whether that had had a bearing on our honeymoon location. And then I considered the will. I hadn't been present at its reading, but my aunt and uncle must have been, and they hadn't said a word about it (and I realised that I hadn't asked them, either). I could only assume they had been afraid to break the news to me that the outcome had not been in my favour – in which case, in whose favour had it been?

I tossed and turned, recalling the anger of the woman in the church – and her arrival at the funeral. An old girlfriend, perhaps? I shuddered at the thought of one of my old beaus turning up at our wedding, and tried to recall how Edward had reacted, or whether he had noticed her at all.

So, she was a mystery, but not one I was likely to solve sitting in a cell.

Another thing that concerned me about Christmas Eve, was who had followed us on our journey to Mean Withering. The weather had been awful, but there had been a constant light behind us as we wove our way down the lanes near the cottage. A motorcycle.

Somebody had killed Edward in the time it had taken me to chase after Crumpet, get milk from the pub, return to the cottage and find myself unable to open the door. It reminded me that I had heard sounds upstairs when I'd arrived back with the milk, and that whoever had killed Edward might have been in the cottage while I was there too. I felt a wave of cold dread stroke my back, and pulled my blankets up to my chin. The thought was too horrifying to dwell on, and it would do me no good.

I had to find out who had known where we were off to – a guest at the wedding who had followed us there, or overheard Edward perhaps? Someone from his past, who knew his favourite holiday haunts? Or could it even have been a passing stranger? The local police had ruled that out, because his wallet hadn't been taken – and that was the prime reason I was in prison, but there was no point in wallowing in pity. Think, Georgie, think!

Edward and I had left the reception early, so that we could go on our honeymoon without any silly shenanigans. I think he was afraid someone would tie a bunch of tins to the exhaust of his precious Sunbeam; a car he spent so much time caring for, that he'd even given it a once-over between our wedding reception and picking me up for our honeymoon! But who had known where we were off to? I thought back to our departure and remembered Sarge. Edward's friend had seen us sneaking out – and he had also suggested that he knew where we were sneaking off to.

Edward had been in the army, of course, and finding Sergeant King shouldn't be too tricky. Always assuming he was a sergeant, and that wasn't another of their silly jokes, so a message to Auntie B was in order.

One of the problems a prison inmate generally has is a lack of communication, but in this regard, Marjorie and I had it easier than many others – as long as I had humbugs.

Thanks to my supply of sweeties, I had been able to get in touch with my aunt whenever I liked, to try to move my case along – or at least, learn a little more about what was going on. I'd forgotten the rules about what we were and weren't allowed to convey to the outside world, but I did know that all of our post was examined, and we were not allowed to receive or send information that would be harmful to the smooth running of His Majesty's Prison. So, asking anyone to bring anything in during a visit, was strictly taboo, unless they didn't know that I had asked.

And I had two ways of doing it.

I gave Marj the last humbug during my library shift, and she woke me up at midnight, to join her for a cup of tea and a bourbon biscuit in Governor Fraser's office. While the kettle heated up, I pulled the cover off the typewriter, fed in some paper, and began my reply to my aunt's letter.

Trying to type silently at midnight is difficult, fortunately, due to my time at Domestic Bliss, I am able to touch type, so a lack of light is not a problem, and I hoped very much that my aunt would understand what I was on about. In addition to which, I was sending it to Cricklethwaite, Dingle & Stone, my firm of solicitors, in order to at least partially disguise myself – although if the note was intercepted, I hoped it would just be scrunched up and thrown away.

Apart from the fact that it was typed on Holloway-headed notepaper, there wasn't anything too incriminating in it, was there?

Dear Mr Stone,

I would be most grateful if you would appraise me of my case, and in the meantime;

My dear Auntie B,

Please do not, under any circumstances even think about bringing me any Humbugs. And I particularly dislike lemon sherbets.

Also, have you found the mysterious woman yet? And the motorcycle? And is there anything I need to know about the will?

Yours sincerely,

You-know-who.

I was fairly sure that a letter that did not include reference to debt, trusts or inheritance, would be passed on to Benjamin and so, not wanting to stick my neck out too far, I addressed the envelope and letter to "Mr Stone". (And there was no question of the deceased Mr Cricklethwaite and the retired Mr Dingle, getting their hands on the letter anyway, but it all added to the subterfuge. And made it look that bit more official.)

It was exceedingly important that my aunt – or really any visitor of mine – should import another bag of sweeties. I regarded Marjorie as a friend, but didn't want to test that too far, by not having anything to offer her. Sweeties were more highly prized inside than chewing tobacco, and a wonderful change from the gruel we were regularly fed. But just as crucially, I needed to know what had been found out about the mysterious woman that I'd seen at my wedding, and a week later, at my husband's funeral.

When the letter was finished, I popped it into the post-bag, and hoped it would be delivered the following morning, along with the governor's order for fresh flowers, and a request for more stationery. (Were we really using that much?)

'I don't suppose there's any way we could intercept incoming post, is there, Marj?'

'We'd have to be sat here at half eight, quarter to eleven, five past two and ten to four to get the post fresh out of the bag, and I think they might notice us.'

'Hm, that might be tricky. And another thing I was wondering about, was whether we could make any changes to the canteen menu?'

Marjorie gave it some thought while she finished her tea, and shook her head – and then the two of us almost DIED when we heard a sound outside.

Twenty-Six

My hopes that this was something that always occurred at two in the morning on the second Sunday of the month, were dashed when I saw Marjorie's face. Even in the slim sliver of moonlight that pierced the office's windows, I could see her look of dread. Oh dear.

The letter was finished and in the postbag, we'd already tidied the typewriter away, the stationery drawer was shut and our cups had been wiped, but the kettle was still warm.

'Get under there!' hissed Marjorie, giving me a shove.

I crawled under the desk, as quickly as I could, and I tucked my feet in as we heard a key turn and the door opened. (Thank goodness Marjorie enjoyed locking places as much as she enjoyed unlocking them, only this time she had asked me to do it. Practice makes perfect, after all.)

I hugged my knees and looked for Marjorie. Where had she gone?

The legs that walked in were not wearing a prison nightie, nor were they wearing prison-grade stockings. These legs were the legs of an outsider – wearing fine, fairly expensive stockings, and they were followed into the room by the insider legs of a guard, wearing the same thick, regulation woollens that were part of my uniform. I scanned the floor for signs of my partner-in-crime, and notice a shadow under the curtains, which might have been a pair of feet.

'The file will be in here somewhere,' said a gruff voice that the two of us recognised. It belonged to a particularly nasty female guard whose sole joy seemed to be making our lives as difficult as possible, and was a long way from the Quaker ideals of the governor, who did at least try to educate and improve us. The guard walked over to the window, and peered at her keyring to try to identify the right key. She was a yard from Marjorie (if she was the shadow behind the curtain), and my breath stopped until she stepped away and turned a small lamp on, shining it at the filing cabinet.

'Here we go.' The guard unlocked the drawer and I couldn't help feeling how much satisfaction was missed by being able to open a drawer or door so casually, simply by using a key. I also wondered whether the governor would believe it if she were told by a couple of inmates that confidential files were being looked at by unconfidential persons in the dead of night.

The visitor spoke next, saying, 'Let's take a look at her file. See if it says anything that will make this problem go away easily. He doesn't want any fuss or bother, and she's only just arrived here, so it should be easy enough for her to be forgotten.'

Whoever this woman was, I didn't recognise her voice, but I had a nasty feeling it was about me, and it sounded like the file they put on the table was heavy. The way it opened, suggested hundreds of pages, and I wondered what was in there, and I also wondered – if this was my file – how long Ivy's file must be, given how many times she'd been inside.

'He has made it clear that it is very important that nobody should know who she is, and the longer she's here, the more chance there is of the secret getting out.'

'According to my sister,' said the guard, 'The instructions are to "see to it".'

'Right.'

For a silly moment I wondered whether Uncle Lawrence was looking after me from the outside, but when I heard the guard's laugh, I understood what the implications of them "seeing to it" were. Then the visitor asked whether the woman in question had any family who knew her whereabouts, and the answer sent chills down my spine – and forced me to stifle a gasp.

'Well, she hasn't had a visitor all the time she's been inside, they're not going to start banging her door down now.'

The two women pored over the file for what felt like a lifetime and, tucked under the desk, my legs were beginning to tingle. I had to get out and move. I flexed my ankle and then my knee as gently as I could, and felt a strange sensation in my leg – a deadness – until there was a jolt of pain and my leg shot out and tapped the visitor on the ankle. 'Wha-'

The window flew open and banged against the outside wall, and while the two women's attention was fixed on that I scrambled out from under the desk, tipped over a potted plant and ran out of the room, with Marjorie close behind. She twisted the handle and slammed the door, giving us the head start we needed to get to the next door and do the same. The guard and her visitor were evidently just as anxious to be quiet as we were – and with the bulky file in their hands, they took a lot longer getting through.

Marjorie grabbed at the back of my tunic, and when I hesitated for a moment at the door of cell 32, she shoved me along and swung me into the side passage that led to the laundry. We ran down, she opened and closed the door and we hid in a bag of dirty sheets.

Two hours later, I risked whispering Marjorie's name, and her head popped out of a large sack, with a tea-towel on it.

'I reckon we can go up now,' I said.

Marjorie listened carefully, and nodded.

'Whose file do you think they were reading?' I asked.

'Didn't they say it was someone who'd just arrived?'

'Yes,' I said. 'They did. And somebody whose identity has to be kept strictly secret, for the sake of a man with a secret he doesn't want spread.'

'That'll be half the women in here then,' said Marjorie. 'Whoever she is, I wouldn't want to be here. She's in serious trouble.'

'Wait a minute! Who was that woman we read about the other night? The dangerous one?'

Twenty-Seven

She was a tiny, little woman, and she went by the name "Edna Anderson", but there was nothing *Edna* about her. Her voice, the way she carried herself told us that was not the name she'd been given as a baby, and the fine porcelain of her skin suggested she hadn't seen very much sun. Whoever this new inmate was, she had been kept inside for a very long time.

It was hard to tell what her age was. She could have been late 20s, or early 50s. There was something about her movements that suggested she didn't want to be noticed, and she moved so carefully and slowly that it was hard to imagine that she was dangerous in any conventional way. But, of course, there are ways of being dangerous without wielding a knife or a revolver. She may once have known too much, but now she was almost entirely silent, aside from mealtimes, when she was surprisingly specific about what she ate and how it was presented to her.

I flinched the first time little Miss Anderson visited the prison canteen and requested a jug of milk to accompany her tea. I flinched again when she specified the exact grade of "done" she wanted her toast, and then when she requested lime marmalade. There was definitely something about her that commanded respect – or protection? It was hard to tell. (And it also made me wonder how much better the food was at Broadmoor Asylum.)

The guards always kept a close eye on Edna, and she was held in a cell on her own. She was never put on laundry or kitchen duty, and I hadn't noticed her visiting the library either. Was she being kept away from us for our sake or hers?

Whoever this "Edna Anderson" was, she must be the inmate whose file the guard and the unknown usurper had examined in the dead of night, in which case, there was somebody on the outside who considered her a problem best got rid of, and forgotten.

I considered my own plight – and the thought of trying to prove my innocence without family to help – and wondered what could be done about Edna, who hadn't had a single visitor all the time she'd been inside. As usual, it was Marjorie who had the answer. She'd found me on library duty, and under cover of Mrs Beeton's Book of Household Management, she told me her plan.

'There's a woman in E wing, who is known as "the Professor",' she said.

'Really? What did she do to get prison time?' I asked. 'Were her citations not up to scratch? Did she give out too many Double Firsts?'

'We don't talk about what people have done!' said Marjorie.

'And if she's in E wing, it was almost certainly something more than plagiarism, bad spelling or taking too much syrup sponge at high table...'

Marjorie put her hand up for me to quieten down. 'Look, *whatever* the Professor's in for, she has contacts and we can find out more. She's a woman inside, who's in the know.'

'What sort of contacts does this Professor have?' I asked – and I wondered how she kept up her stash of sweeties. But Marjorie described a woman whose mother was reputed to have been on the board of school inspectors – or cooked for them perhaps, whose sister may have been in charge of filing at the Royal Company of Midwives, whose elder brother was thought to have been a coal merchant in Fitzrovia, and whose younger brother was definitely a cabbie north of the river... and so on and so on.

The Professor may not have known the people themselves, but she knew the people who delivered their babies, taught their children, waited at their tables, drove them about, delivered their coal and chatted with the staff in the kitchen. As long as "it" had occurred in the city, there was a chance she knew what "it" was. The Professor and her family network had London all sewn up, and if it happened elsewhere? It might take her a bit longer, but she certainly had the contacts required.

I could only assume the woman was a blackmailer, but I didn't say anything. If what Marjorie said was true, the Professor was one of the most dangerous women in London, and not a person to tangle with.

'But how are we going to get into E wing?' I asked, but it was a silly question and Marjorie didn't entertain it with an answer. She had suggested it, she would know how to get there and, as she had said many times in the past, there wasn't a door in existence she couldn't open.

'We have to have all our ducks in a row. No point going to her with half the information we could have, otherwise she'll laugh us out of her cell. We have to go there with intent – show her that we know our business, just as she knows hers. We have to do a bit of homework, then we'll make our appointment.'

I agreed, but if we were to find out about Edna Anderson, we were going to have to get a move on. The guard and visitor we'd encountered in the governor's office weren't interested in Edna's wellbeing, and I wasn't sure how much time we had.

Twenty-Eight

It was Thursday morning – and I had a visitor!

It had been three days since Marjorie and I had broken into Governor Fraser's office and I had typed my letter there and left it in the postbag. I hadn't been called to the office for any awkward conversations, or asked to stand in a line-up presided over by any rogue guard, so I could only assume that all was well. Either that, or I was likely to bump into my aunt in the prison kitchen very soon.

The bell rang at 10am, and sixteen of us were taken to the hall for the ten minutes that we were allowed to see a member of our family, a loved one or our solicitor – and in one case, a smuggled-in tortoise called Theodore.

The door opened, and I was surprised to see Mr Stone (the younger), and I was both pleased and alarmed, to see that his pockets were bulging, but Benjamin looked distinctly nervous. He took his handkerchief out of his right hip pocket, to wipe his forehead, while his thick eyelashes fluttered. Ben looked as if he was about to faint. I tried to rise, to help him to his seat, but the guard grunted at me angrily and the young man's colour went another shade paler.

'Sit down!' I told him, and eventually he managed to manoeuvre the chair out from under the table, and on his second attempt, he was seated opposite me. 'You're fine!' I said, 'Really! Well, fine for at least another eight and a half minutes.' And it struck me that as the prison inmate, I should have been the one being comforted, not the other way around.

'I – I –'

'Before anything else happens,' I said, raising my eyebrows significantly, 'I would like you to tell me what you've found out about my case?'

'Yes, yes, Mrs Mortimer, of course.'

'And before you begin, would you mind calling me Georgie?'

Ben nodded, and began coughing violently, and the guard brought him a glass of water. (And I couldn't help feeling that he should have passed me the sweeties then and got the waiting and panic over and done with.)

'Did you manage to find out anything about the paperwork from the apartment?' I asked.

'Indeed, we did, and I think your aunt is going to write to you about it very soon. She and her office have been working on the case –'

'Are her employees really working on the case?' I asked. 'Her writers?'

'Mrs Mortimer, you would be surprised,' said Ben, and he didn't look entirely happy about it.

'Are they breaking the l-'

'I'm sure that everything they're doing is entirely above board, and I know nothing about their actual movements,' he said a little too loudly, wiping his forehead again. 'Now, one of the things you were interested to know, I gather, was who owned the cottage you visited. We have had a look at the records of the Land Registry, and it was not the property of Edward Mortimer.'

I was grateful that enquiries were being made, but surprised that my brand-new husband had taken his brand-new wife to a ramshackle cottage in the middle of nowhere – that was nothing to do with him after all.

'What was the name of the person who owned the cottage?' I asked.

'Well, as I say, Mrs Mortim-Georgiana, it wasn't your husband,' said Mr Stone. 'It was a Mr M-m-', at which point there was a crash as a table over the other side of the room was flipped, and another loud bang and yells of, 'COME ON, MYRRIE!'. The guards all ran over to see what was happening and, in the meantime, the rest of us were passed letters, photographs, sweeties, chewing tobacco, cigarettes, knickers, tablets, paperbacks and miniature bottles. Basically, anything we thought we could slip down our tunics and hold in an armpit, or – if you were very good at waddling, could hold between your thighs. It was a tricky business, and I watched carefully what Myrtle did, because it would be my turn to "put on a show" at visitors' day soon (although by my calculations, Myrtle had acted at least three minutes too early). I tugged Benjamin's arm and looked at him in an appropriately encouraging manner, and he brought two bulging bags of sweets out of his pockets.

By the time the guards had returned to their places (and Myrtle had been dragged off to solitary confinement for 24 hours) the room was quieter, and the other inmates, myself included, were wriggling about trying to get their contraband items comfortable.

'TWO MINUTES LEFT!'

'So, what's the next step?' I asked and, as I turned to Ben, I was surprised to see how drawn he looked – and how hunted, and looking around the room, I realised why. At least half of the women present were openly gazing at him, as if he were a chunk of chocolate and a hot cup of tea.

'W–well, your aunt recalled you mentioning that a military friend of your late husband was the last person the two of you spoke to before you left the wedding reception. She thought he might be someone to question, and she and her *brood* – her word not mine – have set about trying to find out more. Oh, and the driver's nephew is being employed to keep his eye on your husband's old apartment.'

'So... if my aunt has some bloke keeping an eye on the property, does that mean Jack isn't sleeping there at the moment?'

'Jack?'

'She's one of my aunt's writers.'

'Are you suggesting that one of your aunt's employees is sleeping in a murdered man's apartment, a property that is currently being assessed as part of probate?'

'Forget I asked!' I said, 'Although I do have questions about the will!'

'ONE MINUTE LEFT!'

Benjamin nodded. 'Next time, perhaps,' he said, 'It really is time I was off.'

'But we have one minute more!' I said. 'And I have to know if anything's been found out about Edward's friend, King. He was a sergeant, and we really should get hold of him!'

'I'll make a note of it,' he said, getting to his feet. Young Mr Stone's complexion was beginning to return to normal, and he seemed quite cheerful as he gathered up his briefcase.

I wondered just how much my uncle was paying Mr Stone's son to make the trip to Holloway. I also wondered whether he might be better off taking up inheritance law like his father. I wasn't sure that visiting prisons was doing his health any good, or perhaps it was just women's institutions he wasn't used to. And that reminded me of another question I had to ask. Glancing over at the guards, I was relieved to see them wrestling with Fifi, an inmate who had begun dancing alongside Myrtle, and who was obviously keen for some alone time too. I grabbed Stone's sleeve, and whispered into his ear, 'Have you ever heard of someone called Edna Anderson?'

He pulled away from me, but I suspect he saw how genuine my question had been – I wasn't manhandling the man for no reason. 'I haven't, no. Why? Is it important?'

'It is, but no. She actually isn't anything to do with Edward at all,' I said. 'Oh – and the will! I meant to ask about the will!'

The bell rang, and Benjamin was carried along to the door by the crowd.

I walked out of the hall trying to look as casual as I could, but swinging my arms was tricky while clenching a bag of humbugs, and a bag of "mixed", beneath my armpits. I managed to return to my cell without incident, despite seeing Phyllida out of the corner of my eye, but it seemed she had her sights on testing someone else's defences for a change.

I looked at the calendar hanging on the back of the door, and wondered how long one spent inside, before one began to eye a good-looking man the way the other women in the hall did.

Twenty-Nine

With my sweetie supply restored, Marjorie and I were back at the governor's office that night, enjoying a pot of tea, a handful of humbugs and a selection of half-biscuits (Governor Fraser's secretary had evidently stopped for supplies, and dropped her shopping).

'How are we going to find out more about Edna Anderson?' I asked, in between sips of tea and nibbles of a rich tea biscuit.

'It's a tricky one,' said Marj. 'But we have to have more to tell the Professor than a fake name, although since the file was nicked...'

'It would be nice to know the name of that guard from the other night.'

'It would,' she said, and her teeth flashed in the gloom. 'And I reckon I know how we could find out!' She plucked her lock-picks from her pocket, got down on her knees and examined the unmarked bottom drawer of the third cabinet. 'Staff files, I reckon!' she said. 'Well, it's that or the biscuit inventory.' Marjorie held her ear to the lock and waited for the satisfying 'click'. 'Sorry. I should have let you do that... got a bit of practice in. I'll lock it again so that you can have a go.'

I finished my digestive, knelt on the floor and took the metal picks from her hand. Steadying my breathing, I stuck the first in until I'd found the sweet spot, and let the second find the next sweet spot – and so on. It felt like it took a while, but Marjorie assured me, I'd only taken three times longer than she had. The cabinet drawer swung out and, aside from a couple of lemon barley sugars (which we took, obviously), a bag of knitting and a spare blouse, it contained files.

'Amberley, Buckland, Chalk, Forrest, Freeman, Howey, Maudling D., Maudling M., Morrison, Paxstead, Phillips, Ratchley, Simms, Summer, Vickers, Watson, Watts and Yeo. Any of those names ring any bells?' I asked.

'Mm, Amberley is the librarian, and Chalk is the other guard who reads, so it wasn't either of them, I know their voices.'

'And Ratchley is the one in the laundry, isn't she? Very red cheeks. I think I'd have recognised her soapy smell.'

'Vickers does the Physical Training on a Thursday morning. It definitely wasn't her. She would have run faster.'

'Wait a minute, Marj! Didn't the guard say something about a sister? Her having a sister who should have been doing the job?'

'Maudling and Maudling!'

We took the two files out, and compared them. One of the sisters, Deborah, had worked at Holloway for a few years, but she'd moved ten years ago, to a facility in Berkshire.

'I'm surprised they kept her file,' I said, 'Then again, how many facilities in Berkshire do you know of?'

'Only one,' said Marjorie, 'And it's an asylum called Broadmoor.'

We took a look at the file of Maudling, M. Mary.

'So, she worked here for five years, before a stint at a woman's hospital in Derbyshire, then a cottage hospital in Newcastle, before moving on to Broadmoor – with her sister – and then she came back here.'

'And what date did she return?'

'She returned on January the 26th. It looks like Mary moved the same time as Edna – they came here together.'

There was nothing more to be learned from their files, but Edna had definitely been transferred with her own personal guard on hand – although whether she knew she had one, was open to debate. It looked like the sisters were working together, for somebody who was important enough to be able to assign staff to certain institutions, to keep an eye on specific prisoners.

'What on earth has Edna done?' Marjorie asked, locking the drawer.

'I think we ought to be asking who she is,' I said. 'And who might want her sorted out. I only hope the Professor knows something, because I think Edna's in serious trouble – and if we give her Maudling's name, she might be able to help.'

The next day, amid much yawning, we sat one table along from Edna at breakfast, and talking generally (about card games and stories) Marj and I tried to show that we were helpful, nice inmates who might be worth talking to. The following day we did the same, and the day after that, we invited Ivy along to join us at our adjoining table. We were running out of topics, and Ivy always had a loud and colourful story to share: her big family in Hackney, the time she'd spent at the other jails she'd attended and her comprehensive knowledge of the country's rail network.

'I do believe that them station teashops on tha Cheshire Lines are bettah run an' more eefficient than them ones on tha Larndunn Norf Eastern, an' GWR, but if you wanna reel-ly well-brewed cuppa, you can always bank on the Larndunn

Midlan' an' Sco-ish. No mucking abaht. Their tea is propa – the real deal. NOT THE MUCK THEY SERVE 'ERE, EH ALICE!'

It wasn't Ivy's loudness that prompted Edna to spill her tea, it was what she'd said. I'd been watching her, and as soon as Ivy stopped yelling, the teacup slipped. "Alice" was the word that had shocked her. The mysterious inmate definitely wasn't an Edna, but might she be an Alice?

I glanced up, and saw that the guards were having their own cups of tea topped up, and I took the opportunity to lean over to the solitary table in the corner that, for some reason, everyone knew not to sit at. Edna's table.

'I see you've spilt your tea,' I said. 'I'm Georgiana. What's your name?'

She smiled shyly, and held her mouth firmly shut, until she said the word "Edna". She said it very carefully.

'Are you really an "Edna"?' I asked. 'Only my friends and I think that you look like an Anne-Marie, an Abigail... or perhaps an Alice?'

Her cheeks coloured, and she smiled, until she widened her eyes at me in warning. The guards were putting their cups away. I scooted back to my table, and left it at that.

Edna wasn't Edna at all, she was an Alice – and she was an Alice with enemies. We would have to keep an eye on her.

Thirty

I looked out of the high windows, and caught sight of a cold, grey sky. London is a wonderful city, but it is a pearl that fails to shine in February – and even Pimlico can look a bit under the weather at this time of year. The trees are still bare, and February cold is the kind of cold that, if one is staying with one's aunt, necessitates an extra biscuit at eleven, an extra bun at four and an extra glass of claret at – well, whenever. I looked down at my two pieces of barely buttered, slightly burnt, already cold toast and tried to suppress a sigh.

My husband, the man for whom I was "doing time" was still a mystery, and I had suggested to my aunt that one of the easier things to find out about Edward would be his military career. He had, of course, served in the army, and Nanny had mentioned that "her boy" had picked up quite a few medals along the way. In fact, thinking about it, it seemed odd that he hadn't shown his silverware off.

I know there are some men who won't say a word about the whole thing, and that entire period is a time they don't ever want to hear about again, much less show off about, but that didn't seem to be Edward's feeling. In fact, I rather think he missed the camaraderie.

When I had last seen my aunt, she hadn't come back with any solid information. In addition to promoting Bettina's Strictly Confidentials, Jack's Rodeo Romances and Lettice's Regency Royales, she said she was busy trying to find out about the mysterious couple at the back of the church. She had also mentioned something about a little photograph that she and Jack had managed to unearth from the chest in Edward's apartment.

In truth, I'm not sure what she was doing, but the clock was ticking and the sooner I proved my innocence, the better. I had to come up with another plan, and it was as I was daydreaming over a dreary breakfast, that I heard Phyllida chatting with one of the inmates about her nephew's military career. I'd heard her chatting about such things before, and gathered that the young man had served and fallen at Ypres, like so many others, but something about Phyllida's tone made me think she really knew what she was talking about. I took my dirty cup and plate into the kitchen, to assist her with the washing up, and I learned that Phyllida had also had uncles and cousins who'd all worn a uniform of some sort or other, and her knowledge of medals was impressive. It had struck me that decorations for valour would be an easy way to find out about Edward's past, and I asked her about them.

'Pip, Squeak and Wilfred,' she said.

'In plain English, please, Philly!'

'They're the 1914 Star, the War Medal and the Victory Medal. Fairly common as medals go, they were awarded for service, so they're something he should have picked up.'

'And where might one be able to find out about them?' I asked.

'Well, you could go to the regiment itself, or I suppose you could go to the War Office, but if you don't have access to either of those, there's always Amber, of course.'

'Are you talking about a place, or a –'

'One of the librarians, better known as Guard Amberley. She's a mate of mine.'

I kept forgetting just how much time Phyllida had spent inside, and realised that she was bound to have made friends with some of the long-term guards over the years. 'What? She'll just help you with information, just like that? What does she get out of it?'

'Yes, Georgiana, she will just help you. We haven't all hardened our hearts during our time inside, and that includes the staff! It just so happens that Amber's hobby is working out people's family trees, and if you tell her that's your interest, she's bound to help you.'

I recalled that Warden Amberley was the woman who, on my arrival at Holloway, had permitted me to keep my *Count of Monte Cristo,* and when I found her in the library, and told her what I was doing, she was surprisingly eager to help. Surprising, because I suspected she knew that the man I was researching, was the man I was supposed to have murdered.

Two days later, I learned that Edward had received the three medals Phyllida had mentioned, but there was something else about the information that puzzled me. Amber had written down the details and passed them to me at the end of my shift and, when the bell went for recreation time in the yard, I found Phyllida and told her my confusion.

'You were right, he did get those three medals you mentioned, but the name given is for "Major" Edward Mortimer.

'So?'

'So, at the wedding reception, he was referred to as "Cap" by his best man, Sergeant King.'

'He called him "Cap" Meaning "captain"?' she said. 'Hm, it is a little odd.'

'I assume they met when he was a captain, and the nickname stuck.'

'It's possible, but seems unlikely,' said Phyllida. 'From what I know of these boys' clubs, rank is everything, and being called something you were before you were promoted could be a court martial offence.'

'So, Edward lied about his rank?'

'Perhaps, but why lie about something to make it seem that you're lower than you are?' she asked.

'Mm,' I said. 'That does seem a little unusual, and not the sort of thing that Edward would have been likely to do.'

'Unless your husband was lying about more than just his rank.' Phyllida could be just as hard-hitting in conversation as she was in the hallway, when the guards weren't looking.

I took a lap of the yard, giving myself a little time to think about what I'd just learnt. It was one thing trying to work out the background of a man who'd been circumspect, but quite another to try to find out about a man who had actually lied. If Edward's friends had called him something he wasn't, I needed to know more about his time in the army. My lap of the yard completed, I found myself back with Phyllida, who had Ivy in a headlock.

'Sounds to me like you might want to get your hands on the sergeant again, he must know something about all this,' she said.

I shook my head, thinking back to how little I'd known about Edward, his whereabouts prior to the wedding, and his family and friends. And Sarge? The only thing I knew about him was that he was fond of a drink or three, and I recalled Edward saying that he'd found him nursing a bottle of whisky when he'd returned to the reception. And then I recalled the man's pride at having joined a whisky appreciation society. How many of those could there be?

That night, I went to the governor's office with Marjorie, with a view to sending a letter and, when I mentioned how important it was, she pointed to the governor's telephone.

'Marj! The girls on the switchboard aren't very likely to put a call through at this time of night, from a prison!'

'And they won't have to, Georgie!'

'You mean... is that thing automatically operated?'

'Of course, it is. As you just pointed out, this is a prison! Governor Fraser doesn't want anyone overhearing sensitive conversations, does she? She makes the call and it goes straight through.'

Marjorie was right, of course, and so it was that, despite the scandalously late hour, I rang the Love Lost & Found number, on the off chance that someone was awake, or at least sleeping, in the Editor's Suite at the top of the house.

There was a click, and the phone was picked up after just one ring. 'IF I'VE TOLD YOU ONCE, I'VE TOLD YOU A THOUSAND TIMES, I'VE PAID IT IN FULL!'

'Jack? Jack! Is that you?'

'Who's this? Speak up!'

'It's me. Georgie!' I hissed.

'You're calling from Holloway?' she whispered, and I heard voices in the background.

'I need to talk to Bettina, is she there?'

The telephone was passed without another word, and all Bettina said was, 'Fire away.'

'We need to find the Sergeant.'

'King?' she said. 'What do you want to know?'

'Oh – um – well, I need you to find out what he knew about Edward. He's still a mystery, and the more –'

'We know the better. I understand, and if you don't mind, we'll leave it at that. There's a club I need to get to. Same time tomorrow night?'

'Yes, abso-'

And the phone clicked off.

Thirty-One

The next day was a bit of a blur, as I tried to imagine what Bettina could find out in just twenty-four hours, although the brisk nature of the woman was encouraging.

The lights went out at nine, and I spent the next hour and a half fidgeting, until the moment I heard a knock on the door, and Marjorie appeared. 'Just thought I'd make sure you got in okay – and my hands are a bit dry. So, I'll use the cream and then I'll leave you to it.'

It was very kind of her, and especially because, when I opened the office door, she asked me if I could manage the telephone, and she was good enough to remind me how the system worked without an operator. By the time I'd rung the number, the cabinet door had clicked shut, there was a subtle scent of hand cream in the room, and I was alone, except for the sound of someone picking up the telephone at the other end.

'Bettina?' I whispered.

'Evening.'

About to speak, I froze. 'I thought I heard something,' I whispered.

'You're fine,' she said. 'We've got ten minutes.' And I heard the sound of her lighting a cigarette and taking a drag. 'I had a long chat with Sarge at your wedding reception, and he spends rather a lot of time with the Wanstead Whisky Drinkers, who I've been keeping an eye on. It just so happens, they had a meeting last night, and I got there just in time to catch the dregs of their sad little soirée, and they'd tasted enough Glendronach, Glen Moray and Glenlivet to be chatty.'

I should have been surprised that she had managed so much is so little time, but this was Bettina after all, although I remained surprised that whisky drinking clubs thought it was a good idea to meet on a Monday. What kind of people were they?

I was about to leap in with a thousand questions, but I knew better than that, and I allowed her to take her time; Bettina knew how little of it we had, after all, but she would use every second of it to ensure that she told her story her way. If I was caught on the phone in the governor's office, I couldn't imagine what the punishment would be, but it couldn't be worse than what I already face, after all.

'He has a tattoo on his upper arm, which is the Cirencester Regiment, as per

his company-'

'His company? He was in trade?' I asked, before realising my mistake.

'Sergeant King's army company – his "bit" of the army. They split in two after they were routed in Belgium somewhere, towards the end of the campaign they fought in. Sergeant King said they'd lost their commanding officer, and then he quickly corrected himself.'

'What do you mean?'

'I can only imagine how awful it all was, the man had tears streaming down his cheeks and I almost stopped him, but he wanted to talk. Honestly.' She took another drag of her cigarette. 'What the man said was, "Ed was gone but Eddy stepped in and took charge, and there was a chance we would survive", and I asked him to explain, but the spell was broken and he turned into silly old "Sarge" again. All bluster and bonhomie.'

I was about to thank her for her help, and put the phone down, when she carried on.

'SO, I thought, the next thing we have to do is find out the name of whoever was in charge of the company at the beginning, and whoever was in charge of the company at the end of the campaign, and see what this Ed and Eddy thing is all about.'

'Good thinking, because there is definitely something afoot.'

'Yes, there is,' said Bettina, 'So that's what I did.

'You mean you –'

'First thing in the morning, I sent Jack off to the Public Records Office, and she discovered nothing helpful at all. And when your aunt got wind of what we were doing and how little we'd found out, she told Jack she could either track down something useful, or she could take another look at the blurb of her latest book. It isn't as tight as it could be. So, army records, it was, and off she went to Gloucester.'

'Oh!'

'She's on her way back now, but she went to investigate B Company. There's a pub in the centre of the city that they've adopted, and it's home to some of their commemorative silverware, although, according to the barmaid, what they've got is a fraction of what they had. A few months back, a lot of their more valuable pieces were stolen, and out of what little was left, were brasses from the regimental horses, old badges and photographs of the various companies. And according to Jack, what was particularly notable was that all the pictures of B Company had been damaged in some way. A ring from a pint pot, a burn from a pipe or cigarette. The middle of each photograph had been defaced in some way.'

'Was it done at the same time as the theft?'

'Jack didn't ask, but her next stop was the Gloucester Central Library, where she spoke to a woman called Rita Maveson, who has quite the collection of waistcoats, and who took rather a shine to Jack. And it was Rita's home that she called from this afternoon.'

'And she found Edward's military records?' I asked.

'Of course! So, Edward Mortimer was officer class, came from a well-to-do army family, one of a long line of military men. His conduct during the campaign is recorded as faultless. No record of any misdemeanours on his part, but as far as his company is concerned, it seems that he could be a bit of a... he could be rather harsh. There are quite a few records early in the war of soldiers being disciplined, and even court martialled. According to Rita, it was the kind of behaviour an officer might exhibit if they suddenly had a load of civvy street johnnies in their midst that they wanted to get into line. It looks like Major Mortimer showed them the back of his hand early on.'

'Oh.'

'By the end of hostilities, just like everyone else, the Cirencester Regiment was keen to be demobilised quickly. The war was over and these young men had lives to rebuild, but it all took far too long.'

'There were riots, as I recall.'

'Quite so. Well, it seems that the Cirencester Regiment, or rather, B Company, fared pretty well. They were taken out of France much sooner than the others.'

'And do they know who was in charge of that?'

'Edward Mortimer.'

'Edward... who had been so harsh at the beginning? Well, he must have been well-liked by his men for doing that,' I said, hoping I was right.

'An army man to the core, and yet he was happy to have his men leave at the first opportunity?'

'Yes, it does seem a little out of character,' I said.

'But one of the things that did catch Rita's eye, was the captain.'

'Oh, yes?'

'Name of Edwin Morrison. Killed in an explosion, six months before the end of the war. Captain Edwin Morrison. Same initials, similar surname and almost the same first name, and a "captain".'

'And what do we know about him?' I asked, almost afraid to know more.

'The captain was the only son of a middle-class family who spoilt him rotten, and his father died when he was seven years old. Raised by his mother, he enlisted at the first opportunity he got, joining the Cirencester Regiment, and heading off to northern France.'

Bettina gave me a second or two to take in what she'd said, for it to strengthen and take form.

'If... if one's major were killed in an explosion – the major that nobody likes and everyone is afraid of – one might reasonably be a little afraid of the next person to be given that post too,' I suggested. (And I assume here, that Bettina nodded, because she didn't say anything to the contrary.) I went on. 'And one way of ensuring they didn't get someone just as bad to lead them, assuming there wasn't somebody suitable standing by, would be to replace him with someone they already knew.'

'Understandable.'

'And one way of doing that, might be to take up that man's post, and never reveal that the major had died in the first place...'

I put the telephone down, and suddenly realised I hadn't thanked Bettina for her help.

I closed the door behind me and wandered back to my cell, before it struck me that I hadn't locked it. I returned only to find that I had, but as I retreated, I saw a figure slip into the shadows. Whoever they were, they didn't smell of jasmine and they didn't dob me in, and I wondered whether they had been the reason that Bettina had been so confident that we had ten minutes to talk.

Back in my cell, I lay in my bunk, trying to arrange my thoughts, but one thing kept coming to mind, and I just couldn't shake it.

I had married a dead man.

Thirty-Two

Visitor's day and I didn't mind whether it was Aunt Bathsheba, Uncle Lawrence, the elder Mr Stone, or the younger Mr Stone, Maude, Crumpet – or really anybody else at all, as long as they had information for me. It was all very well trying to find out Edna-Alice's secret, but I also had secrets of my own – or rather, of my husband's – to contend with. My phone call with Bettina had left me feeling odd. On the one hand, we knew more about Edward – Edwin – whoever he was, and on the other hand, I had thought I was married to a major called Mortimer, when it seemed that I'd been married to a man called Captain Morrison all along.

The visitors' hall was already full by the time I walked in, and there was only one table spare, and two free chairs. Whoever was coming to see me, hadn't arrived yet, and the doors had been shut. My heart dropped. It was bound to happen one of these days; that they would be busy, couldn't find the time, the fog was too thick, they weren't feeling well. There were a thousand reasons why somebody shouldn't come, and yet – I felt tears prick my eyes, and I breathed hard to will them away. I was about to turn around and leave, when I remembered that I had to sit down, I had no choice. Ten minutes of solitude.

I'd seen it plenty of times; women whose loved ones hadn't turned up, twiddling with their hair, biting their nails, staring at that door, willing it to open. Given how emotional I'd felt about hearing Bettina, just two days earlier, I wondered whether being in prison was taking a greater toll on me than I'd feared. I lay my head on the table and decided to have a rest until it was my turn to put on a "show", when I suddenly heard an altercation. 'You'll let me in if you know what's good for you! FOUR MINUTES LEFT? I've never HEARD of such a thing. I shall have words with Viscount Hewart about this, you just see if I – thank you. Yes, I SHALL take my seat, no thanks to your colleague over there.'

Aunt Bathsheba was led over to my table, huffing, puffing and rearranging her fox stole, which had evidently spent some time in the mud, along with her shoes. Her skirt hem and her stockings were ruined.

'It is raining cats and dogs out there, and much, much nicer inside. You're lucky to be out of it.'

'Inside a prison?' I asked, but I couldn't help laughing with relief.

'A prison it may be, but its roof isn't leaking – which is a far cry from Ampney. We have buckets all over that house, if Cook is to be believed. It's more trouble than it's worth. Anyhow, I'm here and IF I HAD BEEN ALLOWED IN WHEN I ARRIVED, WE WOULD HAVE A FULL MINUTE MORE!'

'It's quite all right,' I assured her. 'I'm just so glad to see you.'

She looked a little alarmed at what I'd just said, but ploughed on regardless. 'I'd love to hear your stories my dear,' she said, smoothing the purple feathers on her hat, 'but I have things I must share with you, and thanks to those rough ladies on the door, I do not have much time.' Ignoring the guard, she patted my hand, and opened her handbag. 'You received the news from Bettina?'

I told her I had, and she glanced up at me, presumably to see how I'd taken it.

'Right, well before I tell you the latest bit of information, I must give you this. It is a photograph of Crumpet, and she was most insistent that you have it. That little dog is missing you dreadfully – as are we all, of course.' She passed me a little envelope, and by some miracle, the guard standing over us, was looking the other way. I popped it under my camisole strap.

'Now, on to other matters, Georgie. Jack has been very useful. She's found Edward's regimental records in Gloucester.'

'I know, that was what Bettina told me.'

'Good, yes, but we have a question – or rather, I do.'

'Auntie B, I'm not sure we have much time left.'

'In that case, I shall ask away. Did you see any piles of regimental silver stashed in Edward's apartment while you were there?'

'Stashed silver? Auntie Bathsheba!'

'I'm not saying he was anything to do with the regimental burglary, but – oh, never mind. Think no more about it.' She flicked a clod of mud off her skirt. 'Now, we need to know more about Nanny. Have you any extra information about her? She seems to have dropped off the map. Where did she come from? What is her actual name? Because "Nanny" is no good to us, as you can imagine, and we need to find out what she knows that we don't. I mean, for all we know, she might have been the one who-'

'Anyone else I could suspect, but not Nanny. Never Nanny.'

'You're probably right, although I do believe that out of everyone we know,' said my aunt, cocking her eyebrow, 'If Nanny were sent to prison, she'd be the one most likely to be offered a job at the end of her stay.'

'Yes, she would do quite well in here, wouldn't she? Oh, and if you wouldn't mind thanking Ben for the sweets.'

'Ben? Who is this "Ben" you speak of?'

'Ben Stone.'

'Ah! We're calling Mr Stone the Younger that now, are we? Rather informal.'

'Well, he is about my age, although he always insists on calling me "Mrs Mortimer", which makes it a little uneven. Seems silly to – well, whatever.'

We left the matter of my husband's name to another time.

'You won't forget to take a look at that photograph of Crumpet, will you? Baxter's sister's boy, Henry, took it, he's good at that sort of thing and has set up a temporary dark room in the stables. It's rather a good likeness of the little dog. Do look at it, when you get the chance. See if you learn anything.' My aunt looked like she knew more than she was letting on, and she also looked a little sad. And then I felt somebody kick my leg. It was Lizzy reminding me that time was ticking on. I took a deep breath and told my aunt it was my turn to "kick off".

'Your turn? Your turn to kick what, dear?'

I stood up, picked up my chair and threw it to the ground. 'IF I HAVE TO HAVE ANOTHER LIVER DINNER, I SHALL FLIP!' I kicked another chair and screamed with pain and rage. 'YOU KNOW I'M INNOCENT, AND YOU MUST REALISE THAT IT'S MY TURN TO SCREAM! AND ALL I WANT YOU TO FIND OUT IS WHO THE APARTMENT BELONGS TO AND WHO HAD A MOTIVE?' I lobbed the chair of my neighbour, who had very kindly got up. 'AND I'VE NO IDEA ABOUT NANNY, AND I'VE NO IDEA WHAT

MY NAME IS NOW AND... TIME IS RUNNING OUT!' The last bit of my rant came out in a slightly angrier manner than I'd intended, and my aunt looked terribly shocked; I had crossed the line again, and mentioned the unmentionable. My fate.

And then I remembered that the last time Aunt Bathsheba had visited – rather than Mr Stone or my uncle – the prisoner who was supposed to kick off had been locked up in solitary confinement before she even made it to the visitors' hall, and there had been no sweeties, photographs or love-letters passed over at all that morning, and I hadn't a chance to explain to my aunt the intricacies of prison life. I had completely forgotten to warn her of my outrageous behaviour.

As I mouthed apologies to Aunt Bathsheba, I was handcuffed, and marched through the hall of busy prisoners – a couple of whom gave me a clap and a cheer. I was taken in the direction of the solitary cells, and I arrived at a small, smelly, padded room, in a wing I hadn't visited before.

'We'll be seeing you again in twenty-four hours,' said the guard, 'As long as you behave.' She pushed me inside, while her colleague searched for the largest key on the ring that hung from her belt. The room was the same size as my usual cell, and it shouldn't have been unfamiliar, but strange sounds echoed off the soft walls of this part of Holloway. And then the door was shut and locked, and I was left in deadened silence.

Thirty-Three

I had longed for time to myself ever since I'd arrived at Holloway. So much time spent being watched and being part of a crowd, I couldn't wait to be alone, but this wasn't what I'd imagined at all. There was a window, high, high up that let in a sliver of light, and that was it. As I moved around, my sounds were extinguished by the soft cell and I let out a yell – just to see how it felt, but it was swallowed up by the padded walls, and heard by no one. Had I screamed at all?

I sank to my knees and then rolled about on the padded floor for a while. It was badly stained and it didn't smell very nice, but the rest of the prison was so hard, it was a new sensation. Still, I missed my home from home – the cell that Ivy and I shared. We had decorated it with a few of my drawings, and dozens of sheets of her handwriting practice. I missed the bustle of the other prisoners, and I missed being part of the mob.

Curled up in the corner, I had no one to talk to but myself, and try as I might, I couldn't get Edward – Edwin, whoever my husband had been, out of my mind. Had Edward – my Edward, taken Mortimer's place in order to save his men? I fervently hoped so, but without any photographs of the original Edward Mortimer, there was no way of knowing how similar they looked, and whether they had actually done what I suspected they had. But, so many men had returned from the front with facial injuries, my husband might have got away with it. I recalled a small number of old shrapnel scars on his face. If he had marched into the bank with the major's paperwork and his face covered in bandages, he might well have got away with it, especially if he'd known about the major's family, and men were bound to talk and to notice who'd sent letters, and to whom. The end of the war had been a time of chaos and relief, and Edward could easily have slipped through the net. And I could only guess that the men who'd come to the wedding were members of his company who must, I suppose, have supported him in his actions. The men he'd demobbed early. I hoped he hadn't been a total cad – but it did cross my mind, that one couldn't be accused of murdering a dead man, could one? Was I off the hook?

Unsure what to think, I did a little bit more screaming, and some jumping and wall-punching, which didn't actually make me feel any better, but it did change my direction of thought, and when I remembered that I was supposed to be finding out information about Alice, I punched the padded wall some more. I hadn't considered that I would be spending twenty-four hours in isolation. I knew Marjorie would understand, but it didn't mean the Maudling guard would add a day to whatever plans she had in mind. I gave myself a stern talking to and, without realising it, I began to sound very much like my Aunt Bathsheba – and that was when I remembered Crumpet. The darling little dog who missed me, and whose portrait I had.

Unsure whether the door was about to spring open (I couldn't hear a thing outside) I got the little envelope out from my strap and took out of it two photographs. One was of Crum

– looking like she'd just had a bone – very pleased with herself and not as if she was missing me at all. But there was another photograph too. There was writing on the back of it, which was almost certainly female – small, neat and careful.

It said, *"Dearest Winny, We're having fun at the seaside, and wish you were here. Lots of love, Caroline, Caspar, Charlotte and Christopher".* The children's ages had been pencilled in underneath, and it had been dated. But who were these people? And who was Winny?

The photo showed a mother and her children. She looked windswept, a little thicker around the middle than she should have been, as tired as a mother of three would be, but happy. And I was surprised to read that the ages of the children around her were 3, 5 and 6, because they looked older. Big for their age, I suppose. Their hands were blurred as they waved at whoever held the camera, and I noticed that the photograph had been dated. It had been taken near a pier six months ago, in the middle of July. Summer felt like a lifetime ago – and it was, I suppose. Edward had been dead a month, and all I could think of was my own neck. The mother and her children were windswept, sun-kissed and jolly, and by the looks on their faces, they were delighted with whoever had taken the photograph. Six months ago, Edward had been alive, and we hadn't even met.

I couldn't recognise what beach it was, and the light filtering in through the grubby window was beginning to fade. I heard a clunk of metal and as I stuffed the photo back under my strap, the door was opened, and a bowl of burnt stew was shoved in. I ate it, pondered my fate, and – given how many more hours I had in the cell, I decided to study the names that had been etched into the walls. There would be a patch of light on the opposite wall in the morning, and I might be able to see more of the photograph then.

And then I recalled the photograph the inspector had shown me when I was being questioned in Gerald Street Station, before the funeral.

The police had found a photo in the honeymoon cottage, of a young woman. She had been a mere slip of a girl, and at the time I'd assumed it had slipped behind the shelves in the kitchen, or wherever, left there by anyone who might have lived there in the last ten years or so. It could have been a sister or cousin – anybody! The message on the back had been fairly chaste, but I thought back to a picture I had given to a young beau in 1917, as he was preparing to go to war. A war from which he did not return.

A part of me wished I'd had the inspector's photograph on me now, to compare it to the one I'd hidden under my chemise strap, and a part of me was very glad I didn't. Could it be the same woman?

After a fitful night, I awoke to shouting and banging, and realised that the small window in the bottom of my door was open, and a metal bowl of watery porridge had been pushed inside. "Four more hours to go, Mortimer!" shouted the guard. I had four more hours of solitary, and I wondered whether anyone had read Ivy a story last night.

My twenty-four hours over, I emerged from my cell a little more thoughtful than when I'd been shoved inside.

It was rather nice to have a photograph of Crumpet, and such a formal one too, but the photo of the family? I could only assume that they were related to Edward, but addressed to someone called Winny? It didn't make any sense. Had he been given it by Winny? The children were tall – and the woman was obviously tall too, and a small voice in my head suggested that she was the woman at the chapel, but I decided the face wasn't the same. And then I considered the obvious joy of the family at the beach, whose photo had been taken, and the anger and sadness of the woman at my wedding – and at Edward's funeral. An older sister, perhaps? Was I being naive? Of course, I was.

''Ere, Georgie, whatsup?' Ivy was delighted I was back, and within an hour I'd already read her three chapters of 'A History of Trains'. It was afternoon quiet time, and I was on kitchen duty in an hour.

'What do you think of this?' I asked, handing her the photograph.

'Seem 'appy enough. And I'd be 'appy if I was there too. Love a bit of Weston. Been there just the once, mind, cos it's the wrong side of the country for me, but we went on the train and it was super!'

'Weston?'

'Weston SUPER Mare – that's what they call it.'

I turned it over, and that was when I noticed a smudge of ink. I looked at it more carefully and, squinting, I made out the letters, "Wn.-S.-M. Ph. Studio". A photograph taken on the coast, six months before my honeymoon.

It was time to get in contact with Marjorie.

I managed to catch her eye while we were eating dinner (mash, liver and onions), and so – in the pitch black of night, as Thursday became Friday, I felt her tap my arm. We headed up the cold corridor together, to have a warming cup of tea and a midnight snack, at the Governor's expense.

Thirty-Four

Dear Ben,

If you would be so kind as to pass this on to the woman to whom this should be passed on, I would be most grateful. I hope your "enquiries" are going well.

Attn.: B. G.

The people in the snapshot were on the beach at Weston-Super-Mare in the summer. Am I to believe that they're related to the person about whom we know a great deal less than we thought we did?

But why the name Winny on the back? Is Winifred Nanny's name? And as per Nanny, I recall her mentioning something about grandchildren once. Could she be related to them? I hope this is helpful.

I love barley sugars, and I also enjoy the odd mint imperial – just for your information. And no fear, it isn't my turn to "perform" this week.

Do you know anything more about that cottage? It could be helpful.

I hope this all makes sense. X

It was a scrappy little letter, and I really did hope she understood what I was trying to convey, but a part of me just wanted to reach out, after my twenty-four hours in a padded cell. My court case was scheduled for two weeks' time, which wasn't very long at all – especially not when that time was spent in a cell. I was relying on Aunt Bathsheba and her Girls to get me out of here. It wouldn't end well, if they didn't, although "it" would certainly end. I folded the sheet of paper, popped it in its envelope – and shivered at the thought.

'What's up?' asked Marj.

'I'm worried about Alice,' I told her. (I had already spent enough time worrying about myself.)

'I've got a meeting set up.'

'A meeting?'

'With the Professor, in a couple of days' time.'

'Oh, of course. That's wonderful,' I said.

'And what's the other thing that's up?' she asked. 'That didn't cheer you up as much as I thought it would.'

'It's my case. I just can't see how things are going to be resolved.' I dropped the letter into the mailbag. It would be collected first thing in the morning, at about the same time that the milk for the governor's tea was delivered.

'Here – have another biscuit.'

I took a garibaldi and dunked it in my cup, but I dunked far too long and the biscuit disintegrated – as did I.

'Well, I can't help you if you won't tell me what it is!' said Marj. 'Come on!'

I passed her the photograph of the family on the beach, and she turned it over. 'A lot of 'C' names in that family. Edwin must feel quite at sea!'

'Edwin?'

'Or it could be a Winifred, I suppose. Only I assume it's Edwin, because we call my brother "Winny". Winds him up no end.'

Winny. Edwin. Eddy. Edward.

It was a particularly cold morning, so we took an extra biscuit each to keep our strength up, and Marj was kind enough to allow me to "lock up". I waved her goodnight, in the dark, and stole back into my cell. Ivy was snoring, so I gave her a poke, and the snoring stopped for a while.

I lay on my bed, trying to sleep, but the faces of the children on the beach floated into focus; their eyes, their noses, their chins. And I recalled the dozens of photographers that my aunt had arranged to cover our wedding – the sole presence of Edith Prendergast, from the magazine "Blooming Lovely" – and how uninterested Edward had been in marking the occasion. Had he been hiding?

An hour later, there was no point in trying to sleep, and I could hear the birds outside.

Winny. Edwin. Eddy. Edward. Winny. Edwin. Eddy. Edward. Who was Edward Mortimer? Why had I married him, and why was he dead?

I couldn't answer the first question without a lot more information, and I recalled Aunt Bathsheba saying, 'But you don't even know the man!', and Uncle Lawrence pointing out that they hadn't known each other very well at all when they had trotted down the aisle of Westminster Abbey. I'd thanked my uncle at the time, but perhaps I'd known deep down that my auntie was the one with the point.

I recalled Edward had referred to me as "Mrs M", rather than Mrs Mortimer, and I couldn't help but wonder whether he had done it because he hadn't quite got to grips with his own new name. And why oh why had I married him? I'm afraid that was all too obvious. Being one of the surplus women was as bad as it sounded. Of course, some women were absolutely fine with it – Jack, for one. Bettina seemed to have no lack of admirers, and Lettice – well, she was one of the ones who really didn't seem to mind at all. For a woman who wrote romances, she appeared to know remarkably little about the opposite sex, and I could only assume her readers were in the same boat, although I wasn't sure about that.

But how had I felt about being single six months ago? Maybe I am a bit more conventional than I like to think I am, and when I think back to the number of times I tried out my new signature! Being a "Mrs" certainly tickled me, and the idea of living a regular, wholesome life... as I even think those thoughts, a part of me dies, knowing that my remaining life may be taken from me, as a result of wanting something so regular and wholesome. But my husband hadn't been a bad man, had he? He had been there, he had been attentive – eager, even. Edward's interest in me had been fairly genuine, despite my aunt's concerns about him being a gold digger. It had been a small preoccupation of his, but something I had disregarded, after all, his flat in Belsize Park was a sight nicer than my hovel in Clapham. And the cottage I regularly occupied on my uncle's estate was nice enough, but it was no Belsize Park. And those jewels Edward had given me before our wedding – the tiara I'd worn!

Damn Edward, and damn my little ideas!

I pulled the rough blanket up, over my head to shut out the view of my cell. We had made it cheerful, Ivy and I, but a cheerful cell is still a cell, and the woollen blanket hadn't shut out my thoughts. My mind was whirling, and I felt like I was finding answers, ripping them apart and trying to fix them again. I was overtired, and my time in solitary confinement had left me feeling seriously discombobulated. 'Think, think, think, Georgie!' I heard a low moan from Ivy, the bed squeaked, and I realised I had spoken out loud.

Finding out the reason for Edward's murder was the only thing likely to get me out, after all, finding out your husband isn't who he says he is, is a motive, not an alibi – although if that were true, it was beginning to look like there were two of us with that problem.

The young woman in the photograph that I had been shown at the station, and the mother at the beach were not dissimilar. And the children's turn of chin looked just a little too familiar, or rather, it had until a few weeks ago.

Edward had once told me he was good with children, and it looked very like that was because he already had three of his own. And if I was right about that, surely the mother of those children had the biggest motive of all.

Thirty-Five

'Is it steak and kidney pie?' I asked, staring dolefully at the food being dished out, ahead of me.

'Whatever it is, it's not a problem!' said Marjorie.

'Why are you so chirpy? Have they run out of tapioca?'

'It's nothing to do with our food,' she whispered, 'I've managed to make an appointment with HER!'

'The p-r-o-f-'

'We're going to see her this afternoon!'

I didn't understand. 'You mean, we're not going at night?'

'Nope.'

'But how on earth are we going to make it over there in daylight? IN PLAIN SIGHT!'

'The Professor has ways and means,' said Marj, cryptically.

I had laundry that afternoon, and Marj had arranged to swap places with one of the other launderers after we'd eaten, which also meant she was on Liberty's team. (The young woman was a proud pickpocket of some renown who had, apparently, been dobbed in, otherwise she would NEVER have been caught.) Liberty was a good woman to know, and we hoped she'd managed to add Marjorie's name to the list of washerwomen.

After lunch, the two of us went down to the laundry, and nobody questioned Marj's presence, so it looked like Liberty's handwriting was as good as her ability to snatch a clipboard and pencil.

We were on pillowcase ironing duty; a peach of a job, that could be done two or three times as fast as required, simply by doubling or tripling up on the machine, with only minimally worse results.

We had a pile of more-or-less ironed pillowcases all done, and at Marj's cue, an entire box of soap was tipped into the largest "swiller". I watched as the bubbles grew in a plume, smoothing their way over the sides of the huge basin, and creeping across the floor. A couple of the women had playfully begun to throw foam-balls at each other, and what had started as a game, quickly turned into a full-scale scrap. The two guards on duty had split up – something they seldom did – one to get help, while the other was wrestling with an inmate who was threatening to throw another box of soap into the rinsing basin. Oh, and the chanting had begun. Loud chanting. It was either "throw her in" or "throw it in", and I hoped very much it was the latter.

'How are they ever going to get rid of all this?' I asked, struggling to stand upright on a sea of suds, as Marjorie scooted over.

'Salt!' she replied. Well, that explained the large barrel of the stuff that stood in the corner; it was evidently not used to shift snow from the prison courtyard, because that was a job we did ourselves.

And we were about to head to the door, safe in the knowledge that the guards had other things to think about, when an inmate nearby, began lobbing clean and ironed sheets into the foam. And when the woman reached for my pile of pillow-cases, something in me snapped.

'OH NO YOU DON'T!'

'It's just a bit of fun!'

We wrestled and ended up on the floor, my clothes half-sodden by water, and my skin already beginning to itch from the detergent.

'I IRONED THEM!' I told her.

'AND I'M CHUCKING THEM!' she shouted back.

And then Marjorie joined in, wrenching my head back so that she could yell in my ear. 'WE HAVE AN APPOINTMENT!'

She was quite right of course.

I loosened my fingers and the woman ripped the pillow cases out of my hands. They were already covered in foam and wrinkled from the fight, but it still stung to see her drop them, one by one, into the large basin. What a waste.

'Look on the bright side,' said Marj as we slid out the door, 'It's one of your favourite jobs, and you'll get to do it again tomo-'

I shoved her into a cell as guards rounded the corner, running in the direction of the chaos – and too late, realised it was the cell of the woman with the muscles, who seemed to have a fixation for me. She looked up from her needlework and smiled – which made the encounter even more terrifying. I shoved Marjorie back into the hallway and we ran, as the woman was putting her needle down.

'Quick!'

'I've been telling YOU that,' said Marj as I grabbed for the door and managed to catch it just before it clicked shut. I wrenched it open, pushed her through and pulled it closed behind us – but not quite quickly enough. The short, stocky woman who seemed to always have me in her sights, was pulling the door open from the other side, and Marjorie and I together weren't strong enough to hold her off. She was opening the door, a quarter of an inch at a time, her eagle-tattooed arms rippling. It was slow, steady work.

'We're going to be late,' Marjorie hissed. 'The Professor is not going to be happy about this!'

And the door closed with a CLANG. The woman had let go, and we heard her walk away. It seemed that even mention of the Professor's name, was enough to scare people, and I began to wonder what we were letting ourselves in for.

The next door along was locked, and while I shielded Marjorie from view, she furtively fiddled with the lock until it clicked open and we were through. 'SHE OPENED THAT DOOR! I SAW HER OPEN THAT DOOR! SHE CAN OPEN DOORS!' I heard the words ring behind us as we closed it again, and I hoped for Marjorie's sake, that the loudmouth who'd shouted it hadn't got a good look at her face.

Along the corridor, through another door and a right-hand turn. We were entering E wing.

'We're going to have to stop running now,' said Marjorie, breathing heavily from our exertions. 'We're going to have to relax and...'

'And look like this is something we do on a regular basis. Breaking into another wing of our jail and seeking help from an incarcerated source.'

'We're doing it for Alice,' said Marj.

'Indeed, we are,' I said, clawing at my arms. The foam residue had dried on them, and I felt as lousy as a rook. I closed my eyes, took a deep breath and fought the urge to scratch.

Thirty-Six

E Wing is a special wing for special people, according to Marjorie, who insisted on telling me things that would have been better told BEFORE we attempted to enter, while she stood at its door assessing its lock. And, while whispering these important pieces of advice and information to me, she was blowing out her cheeks in a way I'd never seen her react to anything requiring a key. This door was obviously a step above the governor's biscuit drawer.

Marjorie explained that if any of the women we encountered bragged about what they'd done I should show an interest, but neither agree nor disagree. Either way they wouldn't be happy about it. She instructed me to accept any food I was offered, but not to eat it. And she also told me not to let any of them see the humbugs in my pocket, or I wouldn't make it out alive. Apparently, these were the most difficult and deadly women in the whole prison and the ones determined to be of greatest danger to society, and I wondered why Alice wasn't among them. She was obviously a huge concern to someone outside who had contacts, but she was in G wing, with the rest of the middle-of-the-road gang, the women who'd committed acts of larceny and assault, public order offences and vandalism, a couple of cases of impersonating a police officer – and one woman who had even impersonated a judge – but nothing more dangerous than that. (Which suddenly left me wondering why I was in G wing, unless the only reason I was there, was because I'd taken Edward's car?)

'Are you paying attention?' asked Marjorie.

'Yes, yes, I was just...'

'So, which one do you think I should start with?' she asked, as if I had any idea at all.

'The one in the middle?' I suggested, and as she prodded the picks in, a voice through the keyhole asked us our names and who we were there to see. Marjorie stopped what she was doing, told them our business, and the door was opened from the other side – and it felt like we'd entered a different world.

There was a softness about the light, or it could have been that the grey of the walls was a warmer shade. And the inmates? Their doors were open and the guards were nowhere to be seen. Did they police themselves? The women milled about, in and out of each other's cells in a way that would have been prohibited on our wing, where socialising was strictly managed – at least as far as the guards were concerned – and if you wanted to see a friend you had to sneak away and do it. My lessons with Phyllida were the one time a week I dared to break the rules, and they were usually only held when the guard numbers were down, (on a Sunday and Wednesday) or there was trouble to be sorted out elsewhere.

We were led to the Professor's cell, which was halfway down the corridor, and her door was flanked by two younger inmates, who asked us our business, and allowed us in. The cell had a single bed in it (with at least two more blankets than I had), a chair with a cushion, and a shelf for writing on, a pile of books, and a small rug. A rug! By Holloway standards, this was Buckingham Palace. There was no question that the Professor had power. And the woman herself? She was small and at least ten years older than me, although I realised as I looked at her, that I may have been basing her age on the knowing look in her eyes. She shook our hands, and I was surprised by how rough they were, although Marjorie had told me that this lot didn't do menial tasks around the prison. So, she had come from a tough, hard-working background, and that combined with the intelligence that shined from her face, made her a very formidable woman indeed.

'I gather there's someone you want to find out about?' she asked. She was a Londoner, but she spoke softly. Thoughtfully.

'We think she's in trouble,' I said. 'Her name when she arrived, was Edna Anderson, but she answers to the name Alice.'

'And you think she's in danger?'

'She's been brought here from Broadmoor, with her own personal guard. Spent ten years in the asylum there, and has been released to Holloway's G wing.'

'Sane enough to become a prisoner here,' she said. 'Lucky woman.'

'She came with a guard called Maudling.'

'Whose sister works at the asylum,' said the Professor, nodding.

'Yes! How did you-?'

The woman waved away my question. She wasn't likely to tell us how she knew – her sources of information were too numerous to list, and too important to mention.

'We encountered Maudling with someone else,' I said. 'A visitor.'

'Hm, I have come across Maudling before,' said the Professor. 'And what did you notice about the person she was with?'

'She wore expensive stockings.'

The Professor was kind enough to give me an encouraging smile. 'And this "Edna Anderson", what more do you know about her?'

I couldn't tell whether the Professor didn't want to waste our time by telling us stuff we already knew, whether she genuinely wanted the information, or whether she was curious to see how much homework we had done before turning up at her wing.

'Well, that's about it,' I admitted.

'That file was nicked,' whispered Marjorie, and I realised she hadn't said a word since we'd arrived. Perhaps she knew enough to be afraid, but I didn't, and I needed answers.

'Oh, yes, and also, Alice's file was taken by Maudling and the visitor from outside that we didn't recognise.'

'When you were crouching behind the curtain or under the desk?' asked the Professor with a smirk.

I just nodded, and began to worry that I shouldn't have been saying anything at all. How did this woman know this stuff?

'And Marjorie, I understand you're the person to ask if I want a letter sent,' she said, and while I gawped – and Marjorie appeared to shrink a bit, the woman carried on. 'Well, I'll put some feelers out and see what I can come up with. It shouldn't take long, but in the meantime, you should keep a very close eye on this woman, Alice. I have no doubt she's a target, and after spending ten years in an asylum, probably for no good reason, and landing up in here, I should hate for someone on the outside to get one over on us lot stuck inside. Information is power, and my guess is that Alice is more powerful than she realises.'

We both nodded, and the Professor smiled, until she heard something we didn't.

'Sounds like it's time you made your way back, although it is nice to have the odd visitor. Oh, and Marjorie? I have a little favour to ask.'

'?' Marjorie gulped and tried again to speak. 'Yes? Of course... anything.'

The Professor took her into a corner of her cell, and I did my best not to listen. I didn't want to hear what she had to say. Information might be power, but knowing too much of it could be very dangerous, and Alice was a case in point.

'They're safe to go now, Guv,' said a wiry woman who'd been keeping watch at the door.

'Take care,' said the woman known as The Professor, and we left the way we'd come.

'Are you all right?' I asked Marjorie. She nodded, but I noticed the colour had returned to her cheeks, so whatever favour she'd been asked to perform, must have been just the kind of thing she enjoyed. We were let out of the imposing door with the five locks, and we made our way back to G wing and returned to the laundry. Although it felt like a lifetime since we'd left the foam and mayhem of the room, it had in fact been all of twenty minutes, and although one of the guards gave us a bit of a sharp look, our willingness to help with the clean-up was regarded as an act of charity, rather than one of recompense.

It had been a tiring day, and we sat down to dinner in the canteen with itchy, tired legs. The pie was sloppy, and the pastry half-cooked, but it was hot. As Ivy and I rose to leave, Marjorie came over – her eyes shining.

'I've found a piece of paper in my pocket,' she said.

'What do you mean?'

'Someone must have slipped it in there.'

'Who?'

'You know!'

'I – what? The Pr–'

'Shhh!'

'Already?'

'She's quick!' said Marjorie.

'Frighteningly quick!' I replied.

Marj slipped her hand from her own pocket to mine, and in the safety of my cell, I unfolded the little slip of blue paper. Faintly written in pencil, was a single word. "Fairmont".

Thirty-Seven

Mean Withering welcomes Aunt Bathsheba!

The next two chapters are taken from my aunt's diary. I had a short visit from Benjamin Stone, during which he conveyed the information that follows, and although the visiting session ended with the usual to-do, on this occasion it turned into a brawl.

Despite Phyllida's training, I was knocked unconscious, so although I recall the bare bones of what she conveyed to Mr Stone, I thought it better, in this case, to hear it straight from the horse's mouth. And if you think that some of this account may have been doctored for official consumption, you might be right.

The honeymoon cottage in Mean Withering was everything that Georgiana had said it was. An absolute ruin. The cottage next door was much nicer, and there was a lot of curtain twitching going on, so I popped over to speak with them, only to find that the inhabitants were barely articulate.

Baxter was good enough to go up to The Green Man public house, with instructions to find someone there who might assist us in opening up the cottage, and he duly returned with a very tall, young constable, although when he saw that the front door wasn't open, he took a little notebook out of his pocket, and asked me my name.

'And you say that you had a problem with the door upstairs, Mrs Godfrey,' he said.

'No, it's this one we want opened,' I told him, tapping on the front door's flaking paint, as we stood under the portico.

'May I ask whether this is your property, madam?'

'Not entirely,' I replied.

'You partially own this property, madam?'

I admitted that from a legal point of view I had no real reason to enter, but I explained the strong moral argument for my entering and, unfortunately, even when I'd told him my husband's name, the young man informed me that I would require documentation before being allowed inside. He also pointed out that if I got anyone else to stove the door in, I would be in a spot of bother, and ever mindful of the law, Baxter and I complied.

Giving the matter some thought, it crossed my mind that I might rent the cottage for a week or two, in order to gain access to it; it would be rather a nice property with a lick of paint and some new curtains, but I had a feeling that that would be an irksome little process, and that Lawrence would have all sorts of objections. I was about to leave, when I felt a cobweb on my face and, brushing it away, I noticed that it was in fact a piece of cotton that had floated down from the rafters above the cottage porch, from a little brass hook with golden threads flapping from it. And a yard further along, a hole where a similar hook had, presumably, been wrenched out of the wood.

'I understand entirely, constable, but I wonder whether you would mind reaching up and getting that little bit of thread off that hook up there? I'm afraid it has come off my hat, and I shouldn't want to be arrested for littering.'

It was an odd place to hang anything – sufficiently high and out of sight that one would have to have known it was there, but just right for a talisman of some sort. Thanks to the darkness of the porch, the young man was apparently unable to discern the difference between the cool tones of the ivory-coloured wool I was wearing, and the kind of old gold silk with a distinctly regal bearing, that reminded me of the swords and shields that hung around Lawrence's family chapel...

He gave me the thread, and I thanked him, and retreated.

'Baxter, should we give the man the price of a gin and dubonnet? Whatever it is young people drink nowadays – a little something for his trouble?'

'Giving money to policemen often ends badly, madam, especially when you've asked them to break into a property and they've declined.'

'Quite right,' I said. 'Now, before I forget, can you see any motorcycles hereabouts?'

'No motorcycles, madam, but there is an Austin van over there, although it's not in the sort of nick I like to see a motor vehicle,' he remarked, and he walked over and patted its bonnet.

'Has it not been cleaned?'

'Worse than that, it's only got one headlamp, and the Ministry of Transport might have something to say about that. Other drivers wouldn't know how wide you are. It could be absolute murder at night in these lanes.'

'A single headlamp on a van? Baxter, you're a genius! It might be an idea for us to call on a certain police officer, and see if there's more to this missing headlamp than meets the eye.'

The hour that followed was spent trying to find someone who would admit to knowing where the police station was. We made it eventually, and I told Inspector Routledge how happy I was to see that he was dividing his time between Belgravia and the Cotswolds, all the better to find the actual killer.

'To what do I owe the pleasure, Lady Lawrence?' he asked, and the tone wasn't as jolly as the words – and I shouldn't be addressed as "Lady Lawrence" at all, but I wasn't about to correct him.

'Are you having doubts about my niece's guilt?'

'We are continuing in our enquiries locally and in London,' he said with a long sigh.

'And I am here to assist you,' I replied, taking a sip of the cup of tea I'd been brought, and immediately regretting it. They must have anticipated our visit, because the pot had obviously been brewing since breakfast.

'Thank you, but your assistance really isn't necessary. We are professionals employed by the government to investigate.'

'I would agree with you if there were someone in a cell awaiting court whose name was not Mrs Georgiana Morrison, née Wren.'

'Morrison?'

'Quick enough to pick that up, then?' I said, explaining what Jack and Bettina had found out. 'And if that isn't a reason for murder, I don't know what is!

'Learning that your husband has been lying to you about something as important as their identity, certainly is a motive for murder. And it also sounds to me like you've found out rather a lot about this case, and kept it all to yourself, while you were at it.'

At this point, the discussion turned to what we did and did not know, how we might have found those things out, and what we were prepared to share, and I think he was quite impressed with what Jack had managed to find out in Gloucester. An agreement was struck, and I advised the inspector to pop down to Mean Withering to investigate the Austen van that was parked so close to the tavern.

We returned to Pimlico, and on entering the house, Maude informed me that Routledge had called, to let us know the name of the owner of the vehicle, as per our agreement, and I'm very happy to say that it wasn't Edward, Edwin, Eddy, Edwina or similar. It was "William Tucker". The broken headlamp on Tucker's Austen van was the clue we needed; it wasn't a motorcycle that followed Georgie and Edward to the village at all.

The inspector was less forthcoming when I called him back to find out Tucker's address, and I suspected from his tone that the police had been unable to locate him. He also admitted that, by the time they'd sent a constable to Mean Withering to look at the van and locate its owner, it had been moved.

We would have to find another way. I called a staff meeting. The Girls and I agreed that the man was likely to be a regular at a pub, and if there was a chance that he'd seen us inspecting his van, it was unlikely that this William Tucker would continue to hang around The Green Man. He was likely to have taken his (drinking) business elsewhere, and we would need to find out which public house was his new "local".

Lettice agreed to pop into Stanfords to pick up an Ordnance Survey map of the area, because she buys her stockings in Covent Garden. She returned, a little red-cheeked from the cold, holding ten maps covering areas of England as far afield as Hereford and Lincoln. (Lincoln!)

Within minutes, the office was covered in large sheets of paper; everyone looking up the place they were born, their grandmother's house or the kennels where their sister's dog stays when she goes on holiday.

It was Bettina who found Withering, and pointed out how many public houses there were in the area, and that whoever went in search of them was going to need a solid breakfast beforehand.

'Maude? Would you get Lawrence on the phone?' I asked. 'He's at Ampney Tet, and I have a little job for him.'

'You're sending him on a pub crawl?' asked Jack.

'I've no idea what that is, but I would like some answers, and he may have to drink an ale or two to get them.'

Thirty-Eight

Aunt Bathsheba and the Brother

Darling Lawrence returned to us in Pimlico the following day, a ravaged man. His eyes were bloodshot, his brow was wrinkled, his complexion was sallow and he looked like he'd been to hell and back, driven by Baxter (who looked fine).

'What a grand selection of perry they have in that corner of the Cotswolds, Sheba, not to mention their local ginger wine,' he said, patting his tummy. 'In fact, some of the gents from the club and I are thinking of doing a tour. It's about time the Paternoster got some regional beers in, and some cider. Delicious.'

I thanked my husband for that information, but urged him to get to the point.

'Of course, I found out about Tucker, or at least, I think I did. There's a little village – more of a hamlet really – it's called Wither-Withering, and it's eight miles from the other four Witherings, and outside its pub, "The Lion & Lamb", a drinking establishment with a very fine malty beer on tap, we noticed a van that matched your description.' He took a little scrap of paper out of his top pocket; the remains of a note I'd written for him with details of the vehicle on it.

'And the owner of said van?' I asked.

'I made up a story about wanting some furniture moved, and was told that the owner was Bill Tucker, a local handyman, and that he would be along shortly. The barmaid said he was doing some gardening for a lady up the road, and would pop in for a cheese sandwich and a pint at lunchtime.'

'So, you saw him?'

'Tucker certainly took his time, but I waited and eventually saw him, met him, bought him a sandwich and a beer, and paid him a retainer of ten shillings to move some furniture for me in two days' time.'

'Well, that's wonderful news. We shall have to be ready for him then, he may be the key to everything.'

'I hope so,' said Lawrence. 'But before I go, Maude? It has been a long day, and I'd be most grateful for a glass of water.'

'I've brought you a jug, sir.'

Lawrence also confirmed, that the thread I had seen dangling from the hook hidden above the door of Whitehart Lane cottage, was the same type used to decorate the Godfrey family ceremonial swords. Could those hooks have been where Edward had hung the fateful sword that he had used to cut the wedding cake? For a regular visitor who knew his way around the property, it certainly made for a very handy murder weapon.

I shared my thoughts with the inspector, when Lawrence and I met him at The Lamb & Lion pub in Wither-Withering, where we waited for Mr Tucker to arrive at two. He was half an hour late for his appointment with Lawrence (which is not an arrestable offence), and by three o'clock, the four of us were at the police station. We had found our man – and I wondered whether we had met before, but I couldn't place him.

After a little light questioning, the inspector learned that William was of no fixed address, but that he was temporarily residing with his sister, and when he was asked what his movements had been on Christmas Eve, Mr Tucker informed the police that he'd been out drinking ale, and that any number of friends would attest to it. And it was then that Constable Collingwood came in with tea, and said a jolly 'Afternoon, Bill! What you doing 'ere then?'

Much to our surprise, the officer himself not only confirmed that Mr Tucker had been at The Green Man tavern on the night of the murder, but that he'd been there the whole time, fixing the electricity. He also said that the man had had "quite a night of it", and when I asked him what he meant by that, the policeman said that Tucker had had "one too many sherbets", which didn't clarify matters in the least, but he was good enough to give us the young man's temporary address. Tucker was living with his sister, and her name? Caroline Morrison.

When the young policeman had finished pouring the tea, Routledge took him into the interview room and two minutes later, Constable Collingwood was dismissed, and ordered to spend the rest of the day at the primary school fair up the road.

We returned to questioning Tucker, who wisely shut up when I asked him about his sister's relations with the deceased, and then asked me who I was if I wasn't a police officer. (At which point, the inspector ordered me to leave the room and keep quiet.)

By the time Routledge rejoined us, he had found out Caroline Morrison's usual address, and we learned that the home she and her children shared was the cottage in Whitehart Lane. The cottage that Edward and Georgie had spent their wedding evening.

When Mrs Morrison was brought in, her reaction to enquiries about Edward was one of sadness and anger, but she refused to answer any questions about her relation to the deceased, so we waited for a local solicitor to arrive to represent her.

I regarded her scuffed, dirty shoes, her darned stockings and the hem of her grey dress. It was clear that Mrs Morrison didn't have two pennies to rub together, let alone the money required to hire a nanny and get a good night's sleep. Edward hadn't been the husband he should have been.

She was, without a doubt, the woman we had seen at both the church and the crematorium chapel, so it seemed that Edward had had no secrets from her, but could she have killed him?

Mrs Morrison looked so forlorn and tired, I just wasn't sure she had it in her, much as I wanted it to be so.

She had just become one of two wives, which is a firm motive in anyone's book, of course, but could she have killed him because, as she'd sat at the back of St Xavier's on Christmas Eve, she'd noticed the cut of her husband's suit. Edward had appeared every inch the suave man about town every time I'd seen him, and what he'd spent on his pocket silk alone, could have paid for Mrs Morrison's coat three times over. Or could it have been that her patience had been stretched to stabbing point, by the knowledge that her husband was on a honeymoon in her home – tucking into a champagne hamper with his new wife?

If Caroline Morrison were convicted of this crime, her children would be deprived of their father and mother. Would they be brought up by their uncle? Bill Tucker certainly didn't look like he had it in him to raise three children on his own. As Baxter had pointed out, he seemed unable to arrive anywhere on time, and hadn't even been able to keep his van in headlamps.

My reverie was broken, when the door of the station slammed open, revealing a farming "type". The man was covered in mud up to the knees, and his tweed jacket had obviously been used to birth lambs. He strode in, and the young constable told him to go on through.

'That isn't...'

'Perkins,' said the desk sergeant. 'Mr Perkins.'

'And he is?'

'The local solicitor.'

Half an hour later, Mrs Morrison was permitted to leave.

'Is she at liberty?' I asked.

'With the woman's permission, one of our bobbies on the beat took a look at the property in which she's currently living, and the constable has just informed me that they found no regimental silver there. We'll be searching the murder scene later this afternoon to see if there is any question of it being hidden in the cottage, and we'll apply for a warrant to search Mr Mortimer's apartment in London too.'

'So, you think Edward was involved in that little caper?' I asked.

'It is a line of enquiry we are pursuing, as per the Assistant Commissioner's wishes. He fought with the Cirencesters long before Mortimer did, and as such, the loss of their silver is something he is very keen to get to the bottom of.'

'Well, it's wonderful that she's innocent of the theft of the silver, but that is not my primary concern,' I said. 'The murder of Edward Mortimer is.'

'And she is free to go on that count too. She has an alibi, which has been corroborated,' the policeman replied.

'One of your officers again?' I asked. 'You are, presumably, aware that she was present at my niece's wedding and Edward's funeral?'

'As you say, but neither of those things is a crime. And as regards Caroline Morrison's movements at the time of the murder, one of the ladies who cleans the local church saw Mrs Morrison there on Christmas Eve, with her children, and the service was full with a further hundred people who will back her up.'

So, Edward's original wife was innocent, which was something of a relief, but the problem was that it didn't help Georgie. We were back to square one, and I would convey the news to Mr Stone, who was due to visit my niece the following day. (Those romances won't write themselves.)

Thirty-Nine

(Back to Georgiana)

Dear Monte Cristo,

It's been a while since I've written around your edges, so I thought I'd appraise you of what's been happening. I remain the principal suspect in my husband's murder, and it's not just brawls in the visitors' room that are making my head hurt. I can think of nothing at present that will help me in my case, and so I turn my attention to Alice.

Marjorie sidled up to me at lunch yesterday, and told me that another file has been started. I asked her what she was talking about, and she told me to expect her at midnight, because there was tea to be drunk, biscuits to be eaten and cabinets to be unlocked.

I told her I'd run out of sweets (Ivy found my stash and she was feeling peckish and tired after gardening duty) but Marj said it didn't matter. This was serious.

We met at midnight and visited *the usual place*, and she got her picks out. She said there wasn't time for me to do it, and I won't pretend I wasn't a little disappointed. As soon as we were in, Marjorie opened the main cabinet and took out a fresh file for Edna Anderson, and passed it to me.

'What is it?' I asked.

'READ!' she said, as she put the kettle on and looked for the tea strainer.

The new file for Edna Anderson consisted of two sheets of paper. The first was a roughly filled out page of her (false) name, approximate age and details of her health, but what was missing was her history, her dates and any real information. A notice at the bottom of the first page stated that a request had been sent for information from the asylum at Broadmoor, but that had been over a week ago and still nothing had been received.

And the second page, was a letter from the asylum, written on the official paper we had seen her earlier notes written on.

I asked Marjorie if she would pass me another file, and she picked a couple at random. I flicked through them, looking for anything written by a doctor, and I found a letter about the treatment of an inmate's broken leg (an accident in the kitchen – really?), and it was immediately clear that the letter from Broadmoor was a fake. A forged document. The paper was genuine enough; it bore the institution's letterhead, but it lacked all the random numbers, letters and dates that pertained to an incident, an inmate, a patient, their treatment or their physician.

There was no question at all that "Dr Smith" was a practising psychiatrist at the asylum, and that the order to have Edna Anderson returned to the institution was real. And besides, Dr Smith's spelling may have been awful, but I had no doubt that his secretary's would have been flawless.

'They're going to kidnap her,' said Marjorie.

I nodded. The letter was dated two days ago, and it says that a car will be sent for her in a week's time. So, four or five days from now?'

'What reason do they give for her leaving here?' Marjorie asked.

'It says "illness".' I took the file and held it up to the window to get a better look at the letter. It was a full moon, and whenever we could get away without putting the light on, we did. 'It doesn't specify anything in particular. It just says that she's exhibiting signs of fatigue and fainting.'

'You mean they're going to make her show signs of fatigue and fainting?' said Marjorie.

'Exactly. All the better to whisk her away,' I said. 'So, we have less than a week to protect her, and make sure she survives this attempt. Because if the letter from Broadmoor is a fake written by Maudling's sister, then the offer to take her back in is too, and we have no idea where she would be taken. Broadmoor wouldn't be expecting her – because this letter is a fake, after all – and she could simply disappear. No questions asked.'

This morning we had yard time, and I quickened my pace and caught up with our charge. 'Don't panic!' I told her, 'But we have reason to believe you're in some danger.'

Alice sighed in a way that suggested this was not unexpected, and I asked her if there was anything she could tell me that might help us to save her.

'To be quite honest, I don't recall very much,' she said, stroking her hair, and I wondered what treatment Alice had received. I asked her if there were any names she could recall and she shook her head. So, I tried out the word Marjorie had been given by the Professor.

'What does the word "Fairmont" mean to you?'

She stumbled and I reached out to hold her up – the last thing we wanted was for the guards to think she really was unwell and have her taken away – or hidden in the sanatorium. Ivy joined me on the other side and we held her up between the two of us. Discreetly.

'It was nothing to do with the Lord,' she said.

'The Lord? Oh, you mean, Lord Fairmont?'

'No, no, it wasn't him,' she said. If I were a betting woman, I'd have put a couple of shillings on it very much being something to do with Lord Fairmont, but I had to keep her talking.

'Was it his son?' I asked, trying to remember what little I knew about that particular family.

Alice shook her head, and said, 'Well, he's got three, hasn't he?' and then she shook her head again, and smiled shyly with deeply blushing cheeks. And it wasn't fear I saw in her face – it was love! But love of whom? What other Fairmont was there?

When she was able to walk by herself again, I herded Alice towards Phyllida, and told her about the woman's predicament. There was no question of them beginning a *suffrajitsu* session, but they were able to discuss moves that might protect her, and it occurred to me that Alice can't be as delicate as she appears, after all, she has survived ten years in Broadmoor. It's just the next five days that worry me.

As soon as exercise was over, we were divided up into our work teams, and Alice was whisked away. Wherever she was going, it wasn't the library – and that was my next port of call. I was given two trolleys' worth of books to reshelve, but with something more important on my mind, I shoved them on the nearest shelf and reached for Debrett's Peerage & Baronetage.

Why His Majesty's Prison Holloway has a copy of the red book used to chart the aristocratic families of Britain, is a mystery. (I suspect someone meant to purchase the etiquette guide and ordered the wrong book, but then, a guide to modern manners in a woman's prison is something of a stretch. I've learned a lot more about how to carry myself inside from Ivy, Marjorie and Phyllida, than I ever could from a book.)

I flicked through the book and alighted on "GODFREY, William Percival", also known as the 8th Baron Dover – and Uncle Lawrence's elder brother. If I'd had the time, I would have looked for any changes to his entry, but the library was fairly full of people, and I didn't want to push my luck.

It also struck me that if Alice is a "somebody" (as I suspect) then she must be mentioned in Debrett's too, but a single name certainly wasn't enough to identify her. However, "Fairmont" was more than enough, and I found them; a well-connected family with land in Lincolnshire, and their entry is extensive. What the book doesn't mention – but I recalled, is that the current lord is widely known to be a bully. A thoroughly unpleasant fellow, Fairmont's rudeness is only tolerated because of the quality of the hunting in his neck of the woods.

The man's Debrett's entry also stated that he is a widower with three married sons – Albert, Cyril and Frederik, and just one daughter. Angela. She was listed as unmarried, and she was forty-seven years old last week.

Could Angela be the reason that Alice has been locked away for so long?

FORTY

Standing in the prison library, I checked the row I was on was empty, and hoped that the sound of ripping paper didn't carry too far. I had to have that information, and I stealthily "extracted" it.

'What have you got there?'

It was Amberley, the warden who spent the most time in the library, and a woman who was fiercely protective of her books. I looked up and down the row, and then realised, to my horror, that her face was a mere hardback's away from mine, staring at me through the hole I'd made by extracting the book I had just vandalised.

'I said, what have you got there? In your hand!'

'Nothing.' I tried to say the word, but it actually came out as more of a couple of weak puffs of air.

Her face left the hole, and a moment later, she was standing by my side. A usually placid individual, Amberley was barely able to contain her fury, and I flinched as her hand shot out – and grabbed the book.

'I heard a page being ripped out,' she said. 'I. Would. Like. It. Returned.'

I extracted the crumpled page from my pocket and tried not to focus on the growling sounds emanating from the warden. I took a step back.

'You will pay for this,' she said. 'Look at the state of this page – this book will never be the same again! No more library duty and your borrowing privileges are rescinded. Give me your ticket NOW!'

I fished the ticket out of my pocket and, snatching it from my hand, she tore it into little pieces and threw them to the ground. 'Now, pick those scraps up!' she said, 'And give some thought to what they represent; opportunity, education and a chance to improve oneself! And I would like you to put all of those hopes and dreams in the bin!'

I picked up the torn ticket and she turned her back to me and left with the spoiled Debrett's under her arm, muttering something about Elizabeth Fry. And I thought that was an end to it, but Amberley returned with another warden, and they marched me off to the yard for gardening duty. It was a bitterly cold afternoon, and I would much rather have been inside. With the books.

The first inmates I saw there, were Ivy and Phyllida – who playfully attempted to flip me, as the wardens left. As we wrestled, a sudden movement alerted me to that muscly, eagle-tattooed woman who seemed to follow me around, and she was about to make her move too, but I was relieved to see that she retreated when Phyllida flipped Ivy. After an hour of raking, we returned to our cells.

The bad news was that I would have to make up a story for my cellmate tonight. The good news was that I had ripped two pages out of the book. One of them I had given to the librarian, and the other, with Fairmont's address (and title) on it, was folded neatly and held under my camisole strap.

It struck me for a moment, that Debrett's was a book that my uncle and aunt were in, that I ought to have been in, but wasn't (thanks to an errant father), and a book that I suspected, Edward would have killed to have been a part of. And perhaps that was why he'd married me. Because he'd thought I was the kind of woman who could get him into a book like that, when it was quite obvious that his childhood sweetheart, couldn't. She had settled for holidays at Weston-Super-Mare, when I had dreamed of a honeymoon in the south of France – and ended up with a couple of nights in a ramshackle cottage in the Cotswolds, a spell in prison and who knew what next? I could feel myself falling down a rabbit hole of worry, sadness and self-pity that was going to get me nowhere, so I sought out Ivy, and we spent an hour practising her reading and writing, which made me feel an awful lot better, and ready to apply myself to the job at hand.

I had little doubt that a letter addressed to "Fairmont, Lincolnshire" would reach the family, but a letter addressed to the Marquess's Keale estate might carry more weight.

I managed to catch Marjorie's attention at lunch time, and with a raised eyebrow and a nod, she understood that we had important business to do later that night.

Midnight came round, and I hadn't slept a wink. She opened the door, and I got out of bed, and while putting on my shoes, I managed to drop one. Ivy must have heard it, because she yelled out in her sleep (something about the Doncaster line) and I managed to slip my hand over her mouth to stifle her words – but not quite quickly enough. There was a wave of whimpers, snores and "What was that's?" that surprised me, given how loud the prison could be. Were there really any souls within these walls who weren't yet hardened to the random screams, groans and moans that our fellow inmates were capable of? It was a miracle that Ivy hadn't actually awoken, but we closed the door behind us, and waited. I felt Marjorie move, but there was someone out there – I was sure of it – and I held her fast, until the sound of footsteps came and went.

'Who's that?' she whispered.

Could it be Maudling? Did they know that we knew? I shrugged.

'We can't risk it,' said Marj. 'They went in the direction of the governor's office. They know something's up. What are we going to do?'

While we stood, stock still for another hour, our legs aching, shivering together, I told Marjorie about Fairmont and his three sons – and his one daughter.

I was surprised when Marjorie repeatedly asked me what I meant, and I tried and tried as subtly as I could. In the end I told her that I suspected Alice and Angela were special friends, and that Fairmont didn't approve of Alice – which was almost certainly correct. But having his daughter's special friend locked up for ten years? I hoped I wasn't right about that, but it wasn't entirely surprising, and it was a lead worth pursuing.

'If they're special friends,' said Marjorie, with a crinkled brow, 'Are you thinking that he could help her get out?'

'No, I'm suggesting that his daughter having Alice as a special friend is what has got her into this mess in the first place. I suspect he didn't like Alice because she was his daughter's special friend.' I could see I was getting nowhere, so I mentioned, Beryl and Ann-Marie who always held hands, and the ladies known as "Miss Lillian and Madam Rose" who were trusted with the cutlery, but I wasn't sure Marjorie quite understood what I was trying to say.

'My parents would have been delighted if I'd had any friends when I was growing up,' she said. 'In fact, whenever they come to visit, they're overjoyed whenever anyone says "hello" to me.'

'If only everyone felt that way,' I said. I patted her on the elbow and she smiled – it had been a shiver, in fact, but the sentiment was the same.

Forty-One

My aunt entered the visitors' hall, wearing an outfit so out of character, that I had to ask her about it, despite the many things we had to discuss, and the short time available to us.

'Are all your clothes in the wash?'

'I borrowed a suit of Jack's for the occasion, because I was feeling... unusual, and I had a hankering to hark back to my younger, pedal-pushing days.'

'Oh?'

'Yes. A cousin of mine visited New York and came back wearing "Amsterdam Knickerbockers" which my dressmaker copied for me, and we were all the rage as we rode around Richmond in the '80s.'

'Well, thank you for that, Auntie B, but –'

'Oh, and I received your little message about the wedding cake sword, and I popped around to Gerald Street a couple of days ago, and I must say, St. Valentine's Day in Belgravia can be quite savage! There may have been roses strewn all over the police station floor, but there was no love lost between the men and women there. Anyhow, I managed to make it clear to the officer on the door that I had not been brought here for anything the least bit passionate, and was sent through to the desk sergeant, and you should have seen the people I met! I spent at least five minutes chatting with a voluble young woman who had decided to "redesign" her young man's collection of top hats, to teach him a lesson, and when the young man heard – he was on the other side of the room, there was an incident with a packet of sandwiches and a bottle of ginger beer, and my hat was caught in the middle of it. Anyway, I am very pleased to tell you that I managed to find out what was engraved on the blade, and I have it written down. Here we are... "IN HONORE TUO".'

'Thank you, aunt.'

'I do hope that's helpful. And I must say, these visits are becoming quite a vibrant part of my social life. There's a lot to be said for doing something new, and the ladies one mixes with here are quite different to my usual circle.'

'Yes, aunt, I can see that – and thank you for what you found out, but we really haven't much time, and we have more pressing matters to discuss.'

'Of course.'

There was something about her muted response, her earlier chatter and the nature of her outfit, that alarmed me, all the more so when she reached out to pat my hand – and seeing the direction of the guard's gaze, patted the table instead. 'I have been considering our list of suspects...' said my aunt and she patted, and paused again.

I had spent so much time thinking about Alice's predicament recently, I had stopped thinking about my own. I cast my mind back to that photograph. 'And is Edward's first wife on that list of suspects?' I asked.

I could see that Aunt Bathsheba was relieved that I'd worked it out, and a little sad that I'd had to do so.

'The woman to whom you refer is Caroline Morrison, and I'm sorry to say, she's off the list. There were over a hundred witnesses to her presence at a Carol service on Christmas Eve.'

'Right,' I said, with a firm nod. 'Just as well for her children, though. Their children.'

We sat silent for a moment.

'I'm afraid that those chaps who came to the wedding have all been accounted for too. As soon as the wedding party was over, they jumped on a train to the Highlands.'

'That would be a nice thing to do,' I said. 'And the sergeant? Sergeant King?'

'He was the last person to leave the wedding reception, and according to the waiting staff, he had to be poured into a taxi – Jack's words, not mine. Although King could have made it to Withering in theory, it's unlikely. He would have fallen off anything with two wheels, given the amount of Scotch he'd drunk, although it wasn't a motorcycle in the end, of course. Baxter worked that out.'

'It wasn't?'

'It was a van with a single headlamp.'

'Ah! Although, as you say, given the state the sergeant was in, if he had made it to Mean Withering and jumped out of the cottage window, he wouldn't have felt a thing!'

'Quite right, Georgie, and yet it would doubtless have hurt anyone sober, it would have hurt them quite badly...' My aunt held up her finger for a moment's silence, clearly considering what she knew. 'Caroline's brother, William Tucker. The owner of the one-lamped Austin van. He has an alibi for the time that Edward was murdered, but he also has a tendency to run late.'

'What do you mean?'

She took another moment and a deep breath. 'Mr Tucker was late arriving at the Lion & Lamb tavern after doing some handywork, and he was late to arrive at our rendezvous too. It was your Uncle Lawrence who noticed it, the man's bad leg. When I pointed out that William Tucker was walking with a limp, the inspector asked him about it and Tucker said he'd just knocked his knee on a stile on the way over.'

'And what did you say his alibi was?'

'Drinking far too much with a large group of friends, oh, and the electricity went off at The Green Man while he was there.'

'They have electric? All the way out there – I hadn't noticed,' I said, and for a moment I was rather impressed by Mean Withering.

'They do, mostly. Anyway, the power went off and, William Tucker being the local handyman, he volunteered to go outside and sort it out.'

'So, everybody at The Green Man saw him go off,' I said. 'But if he'd fiddled with the pub's wires before they pulled his pint, there's no way to prove that he wasn't the one who turned the electricity off in the first place.'

'Tucker told the inspector that he had only just arrived at the public house when the lights went off, and the landlord said they were sitting, drinking by firelight, for a good ten minutes or so.'

'And when the lights began to work again?'

'Witnesses state that he went back in, and got a loud cheer from the locals – and that he seemed a bit the worse for wear.'

'If Tucker didn't spend that ten minutes fixing the lights, he could easily have run down to the cottage – and ten minutes is all the time it would have taken,' I said. 'And it wouldn't be difficult to look like you've drunk too much if you've just murdered a man and jumped out of a window!'

There was a loud banging, and we realised that we'd both jumped up out of our seats, in our excitement, and that the knocking sound was the guard's truncheon on the table, telling us to sit down.

TWO MINUTES, LADIES!

I recalled the loud cheer I'd heard when I arrived at the public house – and the sudden appearance of The Green Man on the corner, as if by magic – after running along a dark lane, chasing a little dog, in the driving snow. Could it simply have been the sensation of the lights coming on? The building suddenly becoming illuminated?

I felt a joy and hope I hadn't felt for months, convinced that we had found our man – and I could see that Aunt Bathsheba felt the same. 'But what exactly was his motive?' I asked, but my aunt looked back at me undaunted.

'It'll be something we haven't considered, Georgiana. Don't worry, William Tucker is definitely our man, I'm just not sure that a brother whose sister was being two-timed by a cad, would necessarily kill. There must be something more to it.'

ONE MINUTE. ONE MINUTE MORE!

One minute! I scanned the room and caught sight of Ivy in the corner, rising from her chair. I turned to my aunt, panicking and I told her there was something very important I needed her to do.

'Anything, my dear,' she said.

'In a moment I'm going to pass you a scrap of paper. I need you to get one of your ladies to type it out onto paper that does NOT have your name or address on it. Don't use your personalised stationery or your correspondence cards. It's very important. I need you to write to the man with the name "*To-do-mountain*". You'll have to ask Jack to explain – and it is most important that you ask Jack.'

'Jacqueline? Is this something to do with gambling?'

I shook my head.

'Cowboys?'

'No, aunt. It's because she comes from Belgium!'

'Does she? I thought she was Liverpudlian.'

I took a deep breath and, urging her to focus on the matter at hand, I told her exactly what I wanted her to do.

'Well, what a strange request, Georgie,' said my aunt, and I couldn't blame her.

'Somebody's life may depend on this. There are some powerful people involved, and my friend needs help. Remember, "To-do-mountain".'

And I was about to repeat how very important it was, when all hell broke loose. Ivy jumped up onto her table and began dancing – violently, and when Adelaide joined her (on the same rickety table), I urged my aunt to leave, but not before folding a piece of paper into her palm. When I was sure she had it, I looked deeply into her eyes and hoped she would be able to secure Alice's safety. And while punches and tables were thrown, and much fruity language was exchanged, I escorted her to the exit and closed the door behind her.

Gosh, what a day it had been – the mother of Edward's children was in the clear, my aunt and I had worked out the "who" and the "how", and the Alice message was on its way – and it was only five past ten.

Forty-Two

I had just finished my lunch – and the washing-up, when one of the guards asked me to step into the visitors' hall for a moment. I had already had my visit the previous day, with my aunt, and when I asked the guard what it was about, she said, ominously, that I had an "official" visitor.

I followed her to the hall, and was surprised to see Inspector Routledge. It had been a while since the inquest, and he had his back to me. I tried to rearrange my hair, and wished I could have powdered my face, or something – anything not to have looked like I did. Mirrors are a rarity in prison, but I couldn't imagine my reflection was anything to cheer about, and when he turned, his expression told me exactly that. I'd spent two months in prison and, aside from the odd trot around the yard, I hadn't seen very much sun. And I certainly hadn't breathed any fresh air.

'Good morning, Mrs Mortimer,' he said, and I could see that he wasn't entirely sure how I should be addressed, but I tilted my head in response to his tilted bowler hat, and we sat down.

'First things first, I received a call from your aunt this morning, regarding her further enquiries, and she told me about the conversation she had with Mrs Cartwright about William Tucker's dishonesty, and we are following up on that.'

'What was that?' I said, 'I'm not sure I'm up to speed.'

'I gather that your aunt went along to...' he fished out his notebook, and began muttering the notes he'd taken, verbatim, from my aunt's account. I had to stifle my laughter.

'The ladies said that books had to be written – and we all agreed that I wasn't the woman for that job... stopped at a rather nice bakery on the corner of Chester Row... no question of me turning up empty-handed at the home of the lady whose garden William Tucker tended... even with a selection of Chelsea buns, jam tarts and a Victoria sponge, Mrs Cartwright was reluctant to say very much at all... blah, blah, blah.'

While he carried on scanning his notes, I asked him if there was an actual outcome to my aunt's enquiries.

'Mrs Cartwright was reluctant to talk to us, because she says that William Tucker is the only gardener she has ever employed who is able to tame her *Rubus fructicosus*, which are – let me check – bramble bushes. Anyhow, she eventually admitted that Tucker had not been limping when he'd delivered her ham on Christmas Eve at four o'clock, but that he had had a limp when he had come round to clear the snow from her path and take down the mistletoe from her archway a week or so later.'

'So, doesn't that mean he lied? He lied to the police!'

'We should have Tucker in custody by now,' he said, looking at his watch, 'And I intend to speak with him later today.'

'Well, that's good, isn't it?'

'We hope so, although we have found no sign of the Cirencester silver at any of the properties linked to your late husband, which the Assistant Commissioner isn't too happy about. But there must be a link.'

'It would certainly provide a motive.'

The inspector nodded in an offhand way, and said, 'The other possibility is that your husband was killed for his money.'

'But he didn't really seem to have any.'

'Maybe not, but that Sunbeam Tourer wasn't cheap, and it gives us another avenue of investigation.'

'The car?'

'People have been killed for less. We'll just have to see what Tucker says in questioning.'

I wasn't sure he was right about that, but it meant that the police hadn't entirely abandoned me to my fate. I was about to rise – to leave the hall, but it was apparent by the inspector's demeanour, that there was more to his visit than the bramble lady and the Sunbeam.

'While I am very grateful for your aunt's information, I should reiterate the fact that we are the police force, and as such, the professionals in this case. It is our job to get to the bottom of criminal acts, and we would rather civilians didn't hamper our efforts, by conducting their own enquiries.'

I would have liked to have said all sorts of things at this point, but the policeman carried on, almost immediately, in a much more serious vein.

'However, the more pressing matter I have to discuss with you – and the real reason I am here, is because the prison authorities here intercepted your aunt yesterday, with a piece of paper in her hand, which they passed on to me. One of the guards says she saw you pass it to your aunt and, as I'm sure you know, sending secret messages from prison is a serious offence. What do you have to say for yourself?'

Oh dear.

And he fished a little piece of paper from his pocket – the message I had given my aunt. The message that I had fervently hoped, would ensure Alice's safety.

He unfolded it and, putting on his reading spectacles, he read it out.

"Dear Cyril, An old friend of Angela's needs your assistance. As the local JP, you may be able to assist her special friend Alice. She has been locked away in an asylum for 10 years, but her recent removal to H.M.P. Holloway has put her life in danger. If there is any way you can protect her from a vengeful party, she needs your help now.'

He took off his specs, adding, 'And written underneath are the words, *"to-do-mountain"* with *"in French"* underlined, and that's been written fairly nicely, and then there are some notes written at the bottom, presumably by your aunt, just before she was intercepted, that say...' Routledge had to put his spectacles back on and screw up his eyes to work out her peculiar handwriting. 'Grift? No, no, *strict* instructions on plain paper and I assume that says, "*envelope*". Then it says, "*Ask Jack use 3 x typewriters, bin the ribbons, wear gloves, throw on fire. 3 x ha'penny stamps*". It is clearly a very mysterious missive. What do you have to say for yourself?'

I was impressed that Aunt Bathsheba had listened to my instructions as carefully as she had, but I was shocked to the core that she'd been caught.

'Well? Have you anything to say for yourself?' he asked. 'Who did you intend this strange message to be sent to, Mrs Mortimer?'

I was in a bit of a jam, but there was always a chance that the inspector might be able to help. Could he? After all, I was in jail awaiting trial for murder, so things couldn't get any worse for me. My methods might not be entirely legal, but my intentions were certainly honourable.

'I… I intended to send a letter to a family friend of sorts, about a woman inside. She's been moved from… a certain institution to this one, and I have reason to believe that she's in danger.'

'And how do you know this?' he asked.

I could hardly tell him that I had befriended an inmate who liked to spend her time lurking around the hallways at night, breaking into the governor's office, using her hand-cream and eating her biscuits – and that we'd managed to get our hands on important paperwork. And the two people we'd hidden from, who'd stolen the Alice file – was he likely to believe that?

If I didn't tell him, I was likely to end up back in solitary confinement, and that wouldn't help me or Alice. And if I did tell him? I didn't think I had very much choice.

'This woman, the woman I mentioned, she was transferred to Holloway from Broadmoor, and I have reason to believe she was friends with the daughter of someone important –'

'Angela?' he asked.

'Exactly. I just want Angela's brother to step in. He's a justice of the peace, and he might be able to help.'

'And you think that Cyril Fairmont will respond to this strange little message?' he asked.

'I think he might,' I said, 'and – wait – you know?'

'I studied French at school, and it wouldn't take a student at the Sorbonne to work out that code you had set up. The French for "to do" is faire, and "mountain" is mont or montagne, which leads us to "Fairmont", and knowing the circles your uncle's family run in...'

'Right,' I said. 'Of course.' I took the page from the Debrett's guide out of my pocket, and showed him the man's entry – and his address. 'Lord Fairmont. His title is Marquess of Keale, and Angela is his daughter, and Cyril is one of his sons, the Marquess's second son, in fact. From what I recall, he's the only one of the lot of them with any brains – so much so, that many suspect he isn't the man's son at all. He took after his mother. And he is a kind, thoughtful man – and the local Justice of the Peace. He's a magistrate.'

'Thank you, Mrs Mortimer, I am familiar with the breed,' said the inspector.

'Of course, anyway, I believe Fairmont is the reason that the threatened woman I'm trying to protect, was sent to an asylum in the first place.'

Looking at the torn page in his hands, he asked 'And should I arrest you for criminal damage too?', although his expression had softened. 'No more secretive messages, please. And this matter has been referred to Governor Fraser, so you might want to watch your step.'

'One way or another I may not be here very much longer,' I said.

'And one way or another, we're working on that.' Tipping his bowler hat, he went on his way, with the message I had written to my aunt, in his pocket.

'But you'll forward the message, won't you?' I called after him. I received no reply.

Forty-Three

Thanks to my message being found, I was returned to my cell, and not permitted to join my friends in the yard. I was in detention – well, of course jail *is* detention, but I was given extra detention. So, I sat on my bunk and gave some thought to what I'd learned over the last couple of days.

Caroline Morrison was Edward's first wife – or strictly speaking, his actual wife, and now his widow, and I really wasn't sure what that made me.

Her brother, William Tucker, was a gardener, and presumably sensitive to his sister's relationship becoming bigamous. Which made me wonder how my marriage with Edward would have sorted itself out. Would he have spent half the week with Mrs Mortimer, and half with Mrs Morrison and the little Morrisons? I would never know.

William Tucker had lied about his injury, which he had almost certainly got from jumping out of the cottage bedroom, after killing Edward. And the lights on the pub had been his alibi. He must be the murderer, but there was still something that bothered me about the whole thing.

While I could understand a wronged wife committing murder, I wasn't sure I could understand a wronged brother-in-law.

In this day and age, would a man really risk jail – or the noose – to avenge his sister's honour? I wasn't sure that he would, so what was Tucker's motive?

And another thing. The sword. The murder weapon. From what my aunt had learned, it lived above the porch at the cottage, and I was rather glad that, during my time in the apartment in Belsize Park, it hadn't been there, because I could only imagine the fun Jack would have had with it.

During the inquest, the inspector had told the coroner that the sword was covered with only two sets of prints – Edward's and mine. And that was entirely understandable. A murderer who had just arrived at a house on Christmas Eve, while it was snowing, wouldn't have bare hands, if he could help it. William Tucker would have been mad not to have been wearing gloves or mittens.

I tried to think back to the sword itself. Its plaited golden decoration, and its elaborate engraving. It was certainly a very smart weapon and, when it wasn't sticking out of someone's chest, a very fine thing. But what was it that my aunt had said was written on its blade? I cast my mind back.

"IN HONORE TUO".

I felt like I'd forgotten more Latin than I'd learned, but my understanding of that phrase was, *In Honour of You* – or *In Honour of your Sacrifice*.

But was it usual for a regimental sword to say "*tuo*", and use the singular form of "you"? Wasn't the whole regiment supposed to be honoured? It should have been in the plural and, although my Latin was very rusty, I recalled that it should have said "*in honore voster*, or *vester*, or *vestro?* Something beginning with 'v', anyway. One man does not a company make. So, the sword that cut my wedding cake, and killed my husband, was engraved in honour of ONE man, not many. And I suspected that the lack of a name on it, suggested that it was presented to *Edwin Morrison* in honour of his sacrificing his life – his everyday life and his identity, to become *Edward Mortimer*, for the sake and safety of his men.

If I was right, it meant that his men felt, deep down, that he was an honourable man. He may not have been a "gentleman" in the true sense of the word – and my aunt certainly wouldn't have called him that – but he acted the part.

And with that in mind, I thought, surely any gossip about the fate of the regimental silver could be dismissed as mere tittle-tattle. No silver had been found at any of the three properties linked to Edward – his flat in Belsize Park, his cottage in Mean Withering, or the cottage in which his wife had been living with their children. Where else was there?

And when Routledge had mentioned motive, he'd also mentioned the car. And a Sunbeam Tourer is a beautiful little motor, but was it a reason to kill someone? Perhaps – if your own "set of wheels" was an Austen van with a broken headlamp, but why kill someone over it, and why kill someone so closely related to you? It just didn't make sense, besides which, Tucker hadn't managed to steal it anyway.

One thing I had decided though, was that, wife, widow or whatever I was, Mrs Mortimer I would remain. I'd spent long enough practising my signature, and I rather liked my new name. And since I'd been wrongly imprisoned for my husband's murder – and he'd turned out not to be the person I'd thought he was – it made a sort of sense that I should take a name that wasn't his from this whole experience. The only problem was, that I did have to get out of this alive.

I heard the trample of feet and the sound of voices. Yard time was over, and because I was no longer allowed in the library, I wouldn't be able to check my thoughts on the Latin translation, or even discover whether I was right about the singular or multiple honorific on a ceremonial sword. My time spent wondering, umming and aahing had been a kind of balm for my soul though. I wasn't wallowing in sadness and pity. I just hoped that Alice was safe – and that she would remain so.

Ivy arrived back from her little walk and squeezed me in a tight hug.

'Whotcha been up to? When I saw you with that copper, I didn't know what was up.'

I told her what had happened, and she made all the right noises, and within ten minutes, Marjorie, Phyllida and a couple of the other ladies had joined us.

What I'd missed out on in yard time, I was making up for in my cell. It was all rather jolly, and I went over everything Routledge had told me.

'So, the silver ain't stashed at any of them places 'e lived?' asked Ivy.

'They haven't found it yet,' I said.

'And always assuming he nicked it,' said Marjorie.

'Belsize Park must have been a nice place to live though,' said Phyllida, 'There are a couple of lovely shoe shops there, pricey though.'

'If you want to buy them, eh Philly!' said Ivy, collapsing in giggles.

Phyllida ignored her. 'You've always made it sound like he was a bit tight with money, but living in that part of town, he can't have been too badly off.'

'Mm, well, he certainly splashed out on the Sunbeam.'

'That is a nice motor,' said Ivy.

'So... assuming he took it, the regimental silver is the motive,' said Phyllida. 'That's the why settled.'

'The who is obviously the brother,' said Marjorie. 'He was in on it all along. Needs money to sort out that van of his.'

'And the where is easy enough,' said Ivy, taking a bite out of a Yorkshire pudding she'd found in her pocket.

'What do you mean, where?' I said. 'Edward was killed in the cottage.'

'Where the silver is,' said Ivy. 'It's obvious innit. It's 'idden in the car.'

'In the Sunbeam?'

'Course it is. 'e was following the car, not you two. And it's easy enough to 'ide metal in a car. Silver's soft enough that you could just bang it flat and shove it in anywhere.'

'Really?'

'Ivy's right. Last time I was out, I sat on my sister's husband's retirement present by mistake. It was a silver teapot, very nice, and when I got up it was flat as a pancake,' said Phyllida, whose behind wasn't the kind of behind one associated with *flattening* things.

'Um, Georgie, why *are* you still locked up?' asked Marjorie.

She had a point.

Forty-Four

I gave it some thought and, after dinner, I approached the guard on duty and asked if I might have an appointment with Governor Fraser.

She told me to 'Pull the other one!' which, by the tone, I had to take as a "no".

Was there any other way I could get through to the governor for a word, short of breaking into her office and staying under her desk for the night? It was Ivy who had the answer.

'Tell one of the guards that you know who the Somerset Strangler is – if they crack that case it'll be a miracle, and they're bound to let you in.'

'Why would I know anything about the Somerset Strangler?'

'You come from that neck of the woods, don't you?'

'Not exactly. And it's not like the strangler has done anything for years, and besides, if I said I had information on the strangler and then didn't, surely they'd locked me up in solitary for being cheeky. There must be another way.'

While we were sitting, thinking about it, toying with the left-overs of a particularly uninspiring Lancashire hotpot, a couple of women walked past. They were hooting with laughter over their escapades in the visitors' hall, earlier in the day.

'Mary broke two chairs, which wasn't part of the plan at all, but it meant that Theresa got five packets of cigarettes, the latest copy of Time and Tide magazine, a packet of liquorice and a dozen hot cross buns out.'

'Sounds like they had a good morning,' I said.

'A very good morning,' said Marjorie, 'And I think I know a way we can get you in front of Governor Fraser.'

The plan was called a "Jack and Jill" with a "Highbury Puzzler", although its colourful name belied its simplicity. Phyllida would start a fight in the vicinity of the governor's office, when Fraser returned from the podiatrist (an appointment we had seen in the governor's diary) and in the confusion that followed, I would save Fraser. And the expectation after that, was that I would be invited into her office and unexpectedly offered a cup of tea and a digestive in gratitude – and that's when I would tell her about the regimental silver.

(And before you ask, yes, we knew exactly what Fraser had in her biscuit tin.)

Marjorie and I lurked at one end of the hallway, while Phyllida and Ivy lurked at the other, waiting for Fraser to arrive, which she did at the appointed minute. (My uncle would have been very impressed.) As she neared her door, Phyllida and Ivy kicked off with a feigned one-woman-lock, a Tiberius choke and an elbow-twist, making just enough noise to get the guards' – and the governor's – attention, all the more so when Ivy's nose began to bleed. It was an alarming addition to the spectacle, but what I hadn't expected was for the governor to slip in the blood and knock herself out cold.

'Is that plan B, Marj?' I asked. 'Did I miss something?'

'Come on!' And it was while the governor was being taken off on a stretcher, and Ivy and Phyllida were being put in handcuffs, that Marj and I stole into Fraser's office.

It had been Marjorie's idea to play it this way, not mine at all, but I'd never seen her so nervous.

'I'll lock the door behind you and keep look-out,' she said. 'And whatever you do, make it quick!'

As soon as I heard the door click shut, I picked up the telephone. The first number I dialled, was a digit out, and I managed to get through to the British Museum's Roman Archaeology department, but there was no time for pleasantries, so I slammed the telephone down and tried again.

'Hello? Georgie? Is that you?'

'Maude, I don't have much time. Can you put my aunt on?'

I waited a moment, and heard a whoop for joy, and a telling off from Maude. My aunt picked up the receiver and very politely asked me how I was.

'I'm fine, thank you – well, I'm still in prison, of course, and I received a visit from Routledge yesterday.'

'So did I!' she said. 'Has he let you out?'

'Well, that's why I wanted to call. He told me about William Tucker's alibi being dodgy, but as far as his motive is concerned, the Cirencester silver must be hidden in the Sunbeam. They were in it together.'

'Yes, Maude worked that one out.'

'Right... obvious really,' I said, and I could have kicked myself for saying it. 'So, I just wondered whether I'm free to go yet?'

'As far as I'm concerned, there's no good reason why I can't take you right now, Georgie. I shall send Baxter round immediately.'

'Yes, about that. I'd be grateful if you would ask Mr Stone about releasing me legally, with Inspector Routledge's consent. It would be a shame to get out of here and be put back in the clink for escaping from prison.'

'We would fight them in the courts if they tried!' said my aunt.

It wasn't just Aunt Bathsheba's lack of the legal procedural knowledge required to release someone from custody that concerned me. Alice was still inside, and still in trouble, and I knew it was going to kick off this week, it was just a question of how, where and when, so I replied, 'I don't doubt that for a moment, aunt, but there are friends in here I must say goodbye to. I can't just walk out on them.'

'Well, why didn't you say? I can't think of anything nicer than spending another moment in the company of a band of felons.'

'Until I'm formally released, I am one of those felons! And besides, there are plenty of women in here who shouldn't be here at all. And there are also plenty in here who have been released and who then returned inside for safety, routine and a cooked meal that they wouldn't get outside.'

'Still... friends?' said my aunt. 'I mean to say!'

'And anyway, it's better than NOT having any friends.' At which point, I heard a couple of loud knocks on the door – the governor was on her way back.

'Hm, I suppose you might be right. Speaking of which, Bettina says she knows lots of people in prison – and thanks to that message of yours, I almost ended up inside too!'

The message to Fairmont! There were a couple more loud knocks on the door. 'The message – did you – ah! I have to go! Will you see what you can do?' I asked. I slammed the phone down, scampered out of the room, and I was halfway down the corridor before I dared speak. 'I can't believe we got away with that!'

'We did. Ivy and Phyllida didn't!' said Marjorie.

'Oh!'

'It's all right. They helped cart Fraser off to the sanatorium, and I overheard her say something about them being gentler than the guards were. They won't be in long. A couple of hours at most.'

I could have kicked myself for not mentioning the message about Alice earlier in the call, and I just hoped that Routledge had done something. Outside the prison walls, he was our only hope.

We returned to my cell and sat together on my bunk in silence, reflecting on the fact that I would need no more humbugs, chocolate limes, or mint imperials to ensure my survival. My aunt no longer had to schlep her way over to Holloway. There were no more plans to be hatched, no more secrets to dig up. I would be taken off the roster for visiting hall riots – no longer responsible for ensuring enough mayhem that the many small, life-saving transactions that made life inside bearable, were conducted while the guards attempted to calm things down. Twists of paper covered in news from home, drawings by children, drawings for children, and photographs of the children that the women inside wouldn't see from one birthday to the next, sweeties – of course – and cigarettes and chewing tobacco with which to while away the many hours of boredom.

And I certainly would not miss the boredom, or the low-level buzz of menace that pervaded the place.

Ivy had been a friend, a guide to life inside and a project. Her reading was coming along nicely. Marjorie had made my nights a lot more interesting – and added a string to my bow. And Phyllida had too, of course. She'd certainly made me feel safer, but not exactly safe.

Although, when I thought about it, I had to admit, that I hadn't seen a visitor riot that had ended as badly as the first one I'd witnessed – and been a party to. I stroked my slightly wonky nose in contemplation.

Forty-Five

Dear Monte Cristo,

I'm not sure how long I have left in Holloway – a couple of hours, a day, a week? Every time a guard walks by, I expect her to tell me that I'm free to go, and then present me with a bag of colourful clothes and a hall pass out of here.

I told Ivy about my meeting with Auntie B earlier; that I may be leaving soon. Although she spent the next hour sobbing, she assured me she was happy for me and asked if I could find somebody willing to pay for the 25 pairs of shoes Phyllida hadn't paid for. I told her that the law doesn't work like that, and also that I suspect that Phyllida – who is generally barefoot – did the shoplifting in order to get back in. She is a woman who loves nothing more than an impromptu fight, followed by an earnest lesson in the art of self-defence, with a bit of offence on the side. Those aren't pastimes that are easily found on the outside; she isn't going anywhere, and it doesn't seem right for *Messrs Anello & Davide* to have to pay the price every time she wants to see her mates or teach a class.

My cellmate and I have spent every spare moment reading together since I arrived, and if we could only get our hands on a paper, Ivy would be reading the cartoons in the Express by now, but there are so few copies, by the time they get to our wing, the funnies are long gone. She could be out within a couple of years, and I have promised her that if she hasn't moved on to the Four Musketeers by then, I will sit down and read it to her. No, dear diary, I do not see *The Count of Monte Cristo* in her sights – you are at least a thousand pages too long, there are too many characters and there is just too much going on.

Marjorie has been happy to have a friend to enjoy an illicit cuppa with, but I suspect she is happier on her own, generally. Whenever we go on a tea spree, she is very encouraging on the letter-writing and file-finding front, and a part of me wonders whether, because of our shared secret, she considers me a bit of a liability. If only my lock-picking were quicker.

And Alice?

I only hope that Inspector Routledge did the right thing, and contacted Cyril about his sister's special friend. I have my eyes on her but, more to the point, Marj and I have our eyes on the guard we encountered in the office – the elder Maudling sister, not to mention the inmate who I feel sure has been following me around since the moment I arrived. The short woman whose intense gaze and muscular arms worry me.

All in all, I can't help feeling I have had enough of mysterious women in general, what with the woman at the wedding, the woman at the funeral and the woman in those photographs, and the two women who visited the governor's office, not to mention Nanny, the jasmine-scented woman (Marj), Edna who was Alice, and now this one with the tattooed biceps. And that doesn't include all the slightly dodgy women who prowl around and on whom one has to keep a casually close eye if one is to survive (as per Phyllida's instructions). More later. That was the bell for lunch.

Half of the hall were eating, and half were lining up waiting for their pie. I was at one end of the hall, and Edna-Alice was seated at the other end, at her usual table, when I saw her crumple up in a heap. She was immediately attended to by one of the guards, which would have been a comfort, if it hadn't been for Guard Maudling rushing over and assuring her colleagues that she would take charge, and even from the other end of the room, I could tell that Maudling was anxious to take over. Alice was dragged away, and it was imperative I follow.

I bashed my way through the crowd, but could not get any headway, and realised there was only one way I could separate the room. I grabbed a handful of mashed potato off a nearby inmate's plate, and chucked it in the direction of the queue. Half of the inmates dove under tables, and the other half prepared for the fracas by tipping up a huge pan of potato on the counter. The hall had divided, and I ran through, keen to see how Alice was, but had they gone left or right? I heard a muffled groan and followed. We were moving in the direction of the infirmary and when I reached the medical bay's double doors, I struggled to open them – until I heard another groan from the corridor ahead of me, and realised that Guard Maudling was taking Alice to solitary confinement.

As I ran, it suddenly struck me that I didn't know what I was going to do when I reached them, and turning a corner, that moment arrived. Alice looked pale and confused, and with her eyes rolling, and her chest rising and falling with heavy breathing, she was held fast by the guard, who was backing her way into another corridor.

'STOP RIGHT THERE!' she hissed, dragging the woman back with her. Maudling had her hands around Alice's neck, and as I stumbled forward, they got a little tighter. What could I do?

As the two of them slipped through the door, there was a loud gurgling sound, and I looked to Alice, but her colour seemed to have improved, if anything. Then I looked up at Maudling, who had turned purple – and who had hands around her own neck. What? The inmate and the guard were pushed forward, out of the doors they'd been backing into, and Alice was released. As she fell to the floor, Maudling remained upright, and in the hands of – of the woman whose gaze I'd spent so much time avoiding. The short, muscular woman with the eagle tattoo on her arm.

'Orright?' she asked.

I nodded, unsure what to do.

'You might wanna get 'er some 'elp while I deal wiv this one,' she said. 'An' it was Betty – sorry, "Bettina" what asked me to keep a look out for ya.'

I nodded again, doing everything I could to stay upright as my knees began to buckle, and the woman reversed through the doors, with the guard in her firm, bulging grip.

I helped Alice to her feet, the two of us made our way to sickbay for a check-up, and I wondered (not for the first time) where Bettina found her friends.

While I waited to find out how Alice was, a small party arrived, led by Governor Fraser. One of the men in the group seemed familiar, and when the governor told the matron on call that the gentleman wished to question the patient – and that he was a magistrate, I rose from my chair to introduce myself to Cyril Fairmont. And as I took a step forward and held out my hand, my Aunt Bathsheba came to mind, and I imagined the look on her face if word of my incarceration were to get out. I withdrew and slipped into the corridor. Inspector Routledge had passed the message on, after all. Alice was in safe hands – and perhaps my secret was too.

Forty-Six

To be anyone's second choice isn't ideal, but to be the second wife when the first is still around, is not to be recommended, unless you want to be read about in the papers. With only a couple of days before I was assured my release would be made official, I was permitted a bundle of Gazettes, Times and Standards to peruse, thanks to my uncle.

And I suspect it was also thanks to him, that the reports about my brief marriage with Edward made no mention of bigamy, and the papers published Edwin Morrison's crimes under the name "Edward Morrison" thereby assigning them to neither man. A welcome misunderstanding.

I still had questions. Why Edwin had chosen to take on Edward's identity so fully, when he could have waited to see if he was promoted to the next rank up? And why he had left his family behind? A confused attempt to impress Nanny? (Who hadn't seemed in the least bit impressed by me.) A way to make some money? There were no easy answers. He had evidently spent the three weeks before our wedding with his wife and children, which was some consolation to them, I suppose. But that family had lost a father – and now, an uncle.

It was William Tucker who'd been sitting at the back of the church, beside the scowling woman in black, who was my husband's first wife. And from there he had followed us all the way to Mean Withering, bungled The Green Man's electrics, run down to Whitehart Lane Cottage, made a mess looking for the silver, murdered Edward, jumped out of the bedroom window, made it back up to the pub, rejigged their wires and loudly ordered a pint – all while I was chasing the dog in the snow. And when I'd turned up, he'd tried to order me a drink too.

Tucker had certainly made enough noise to make everyone remember he was there and, by the end of the night, his limp would have been mistaken for drunken stumbling.

I tried not to think about what would have happened if Crumpet hadn't led me a merry dance up and down the lanes, while I went in search of milk for my new husband's tea.

And the man's motive? To retrieve his share of the regimental silver. He and Edward Mortimer had stolen it together, and stored it in the cottage in Whitehart Lane, unbeknownst to Caroline. And when Edward had moved wife no.1 out of the cottage, he had stashed it in the underside of the Sunbeam, which might have accounted for its heavy steering. Neither my aunt nor I had found out what his plans for the treasure were, and Tucker claimed he'd never meant to kill Edward, just talk to him, although that was up to the police to investigate now. But, according to my aunt, William Tucker's cause hadn't been helped by an impassioned outburst he'd made, which had shown just how aggrieved he was to see the money Edward had spent on his car and clothes, since abandoning his sister and her children to their dismal little cottage.

As for the original Edward Mortimer, his family had died long before the war, thus giving Edwin the opportunity to pull off the deception. Needless to say, Edwin's family consisted of Nanny, who was of course his own mother – and grandmother to his three children. That she had disapproved of my arrival on the scene was understandable, but it had been her son's decision to become a bigamist, not mine to marry one.

It seemed that the young wife Edwin Morrison had when he left for war, wasn't the woman he had in mind as he took on the persona of Edward Mortimer. And I suppose on paper, I suited his idea of the perfect Mrs Mortimer. How little he knew. Bettina had suggested he was looking for someone who would look the part, if he were to take up a political career, but it just didn't make sense. So many people were privy to his secret. The only fathomable reason was that he thought I had money, because of my distantly-aristocratic uncle and aunt. (My matador-loving mother must have come as a bit of a shock to him!)

I had assured my auntie that there was no need for her to visit Holloway again while we waited for the paperwork to be settled for my release. I could manage one last visitor session without her, but she told me it was no trouble, and so, when 10am came around, she arrived – the first to enter the hall and, taking her seat, she asked me what my plans were when I got out.

'I'd like to sell Edward – Edwin's flat, get my old job back and just get back to normal,' I said.

'Normal?' she asked, 'Hm, well I've arranged a meeting with Mr Stone about that, and he should be here any minute... now?' She cocked her head, and nothing happened. Eight seconds later, the door to the visiting hall opened, and he appeared.

I was disappointed to see the elder Mr Stone come to the table, and when Aunt Bathsheba asked after his son, he explained that the young man was sitting his bar exams.

'Sitting his exams?' I asked, hoping that I'd misheard what he'd said.

'Yes. He has his last one today.'

'His last bar exam is... today? You mean to say that all the time I've spent in prison, I thought I was being visited by a fully-qualified solicitor, and I was actually being advised by a-a-a student?'

'A very good student,' said Mr Stone, 'He is at the top of his class, and one must get one's experience somewhere. It's not easy.'

'It's a lot easier than being in prison!'

While my aunt patiently assured me that I had had a very interesting time inside, Mr Stone unloaded files from his attaché case, and when he had a pile of four or five of them, he took his seat again.

'It is very good of you to bring all of that over, Mr Stone, but I don't think I need to see the evidence of whatever you're about to tell me, or any of the actual details about the will,' I said, 'If you could just give me the basics an-' and Aunt Bathsheba looked at me as only the wife of a parliamentary report-publisher can. (She likes to pretend Lawrence's business is a hobby, and that it's beneath her, but I suspect she has a fairly firm grasp of things.)

'Please, go ahead, Stone,' she said, offering me a pear drop, to keep me quiet, and I sucked thoughtfully for the next two-and-a-half minutes.

Forty-Seven

'So, what you're trying to tell us is that the wedding doesn't count, that Georgiana was never married to this bounder.'

'Correct.'

'But that's rather good, isn't it?'

'Good for Mrs – Miss – good for her as far as the records go…'

And Mr Stone ignored my aunt when she asked if he was absolutely sure about all this – it being something other than inheritance duty.

'And the apartment?' I asked.

'Your late husband had that listed under his false name too. He wrote his will under the name "Edward Mortimer", and it is the name he lived under when he died, and a little investigation has indicated that the property was purchased with a deposit of combined moneys from Captain Morrison and Major Mortimer's estate.'

'So?' said my aunt.

'So, with a bit of wrangling, a certain percentage of the apartment might have been yours, but –'

Bathsheba beamed. 'Jolly good. It is a lovely little property that.' My aunt seemed not to have caught the conditional nature of the sentence, and with a flourish of her handkerchief, she went on. 'When you're released, you are, of course, very welcome to carry on staying in the cottage in Ampney whenever you're in the Cotswolds – or stay in the townhouse in Pimlico, which is so very grand and spacious, but it would be super to have a place uptown too. Maude would enjoy that little challenge, I'm sure.'

For a moment, I imagined I could hear the distant sound of Maude juggling porcelain and some rather fruity language. My aunt wouldn't have recognised a feather duster at five paces and had no idea how much work went into keeping just one home clean, let alone two, without the trouble of a third.

'You mentioned a "might" and a "but", Mr Stone,' I said.

'The apartment wasn't your late husband's either, I'm afraid.'

'But Edward said –!'

'I'm afraid it wasn't his. Neither Mr Morrison nor Mr Mortimer kept up the loan payments.'

'Oh.'

'So... so he was penniless?' said my aunt, and her hat drooped a bit.

I had lost my philandering, dishonest husband, my married title and name, and the lovely little apartment. And it looked like I was back to being Georgie Wren. No more Mrs for me, although the wedding ring might come in handy now and again, and I could always sell my engagement ring if times got tough. I wasn't the owner of a swanky flat in Belsize Park. I wasn't the owner of anything. Or was I?

'What about the car?' I asked.

'The car?'

'The Sunbeam Tourer. Whose name is that registered in?'

'Ah, now that is also registered in your husband's name, at the address in Withering, and he owned the car in its entirety. Won it in a game, as far as we can tell. Got it from a Sergeant Jeremy Arnold King who lives in Wimbledon – according to my records.'

If we had only looked at the car's paperwork, we would have found out a lot of information, much earlier than we had. But I couldn't help feeling that, Crumpet aside of course, I should take one souvenir with me from my unfortunate marriage. And the Sunbeam really was the least I deserved, seeing as my driving my dead husband's car back to town was what had ensured I was locked up prior to the trial. And I told Mr Stone as much.

'Yes,' he said, 'And I can see how you would feel that way, but I'm afraid that, as the second wife to a fictitious man, you aren't entitled to any of his estate. Howev-'

'Pooh!' said my aunt. 'Nothing?'

'- however, I have spoken with your uncle, and he has suggested that he purchase the car from Mrs Morrison, for your use. The chauffeur, Baxter, said that the vehicle in question wasn't best suited to life in...' He looked through his notes.

'Mean Withering,' I said. The thought of Mrs Morrison and her three children living in the middle of nowhere, in debt, after years of little or no husband and a lifetime of holidays in Weston-Super-Mare made my blood freeze. Edward – Edwin – whatever his name was, my husband hadn't had two pennies to rub together. The needs of Mrs Morrison were greater than mine, however much I liked the look of the shoes I'd seen in Selfridges' November window. And a Sunbeam Tourer was a hell of a car.

'Oh, and Baxter has given it a test drive and apparently it handles much better since the police removed the regimental silver from certain parts of its undercarriage.'

'Well, that is good news – and very kind of Uncle Lawrence.' My aunt absent-mindedly patted my arm, but she was evidently thinking about the apartment that was no more.

'ONE AND A HALF MINUTES TO GO, LADIES!'

On my advice, Mr Stone rose to leave the visiting room with a minute to spare before it was Phyllida's turn to start a small riot. She was bound to put on quite a show. And it was particularly important this week, because one of the women was expecting a photograph of her new grandson and, as Phyllida pointed out, it was one thing being shown a picture at a distance, but quite another for the incarcerated grandmother to be able to look at the little baby's face every night before bed.

The visitor's entrance door clicked shut behind Mr Stone, and I turned to my aunt. 'I do hope "Domestic Bliss" will have me back,' I said.

'You may be single again,' said my aunt, 'But I doubt that "widowed inmate accused of murder" is the image that a magazine for young wives is looking for.'

'But we weren't legally married, Auntie Sheba!' I protested, 'And I shall be free in the morning!'

'Guilty or not, you are still an ex-con,' said my aunt, 'They'd be more likely to employ Crumpet.' She patted my hand firmly. 'Try not to worry about it, Georgie, there may be an opening for you in my little publishing organisation. We shall have to have a chat about it when I see you next, my dear.'

And with that, my aunt weaved her way out of the hall, between the flying insults, chair-legs and sweeties. I would see her tomorrow.

Forty-Eight

My last – and first morning

After a teary farewell to the ladies, I picked up my *Count of Monte Cristo*, and a guard escorted me to the registration office, where my grey linen pinafore and thick woollen stockings were swapped for the contents of a paper bag.

I was given five minutes alone, to change into the black skirt, cardigan and stockings, lace-up shoes and coat that I'd worn when I'd entered the prison. Widow's weeds they might have been, but the softness of the cashmere, velvet and silk almost took my breath away and, just for a moment, I was overwhelmed by the thought of going back to a world in which such fineries existed.

My departure from H.M.P. Holloway was marked with as little ceremony as my arrival had been, and with no further ado, the small door encased within the broad wood of the prison's imposing gates was unlocked, and a bright, breezy blue sky was revealed. Holding the door open for me, the guard bid me goodbye, with a stern 'And don't let us see you in here again,', and I was about to cross the threshold when my arm was tapped, and I was passed a telegram. It was addressed to "Mrs E. Mortimer."

Edward was no longer a part of my life, but I mused that I might just hang on to my title and name. It hadn't actually been my husband's, after all.

Mrs Mortimer.

A new name, a new me – but what next? I stepped outside, and ripped open the telegram to find out.

ACKNOWLEDGEMENTS

Thank you to Stuart for his love, encouragement and suggestions; to Tristan for his literary and artistic help; and to James for his technical support.

Thank you to Mater, the Lawrences and the Clarks for their enthusiasm, help, excitement, encouragement, suggestions, questions and general loveliness. I know Dad would have liked the Sunbeam.

And thank you to Ruth and Lyn for being such good chums! Tea, anyone?

And to you, dear reader, thank you for reading the account of Mrs Mortimer's ill-fated wedding and her incarceration.

I hope you enjoyed it, and I would be most grateful if you would leave a review wherever you buy your books.

It should be said, authors love reviews almost as much as Bathsheba loves a fresh pot of tea. Or a small sherry.

Georgiana's next adventures are

"Death in Heels"
"Death in Tweed"

and **"Death First Class"** (coming soon).

If you would like to know how Bathsheba met her ladies, pop along to my website, **eeoakeyauthor.com**, to sign up for **"Death Off Season".**

It is a free-to-download novella - and very good fun.

And to find out more about me or Mrs Mortimer, we can be found on Instagram and FB, as **eeoakeyauthor**.

Printed in Great Britain
by Amazon

24151914R00142